Solution T

Also by Naomi Mitchison

SOLUTION THREE

By Naomi Mitchison
Afterword by Susan M. Squier

The Feminist Press at The City University of New York
New York

To Jim Watson, who first suggested this horrid idea

Published 1995 by The Feminist Press at The City University of New York,
311 East 94 Street, New York, NY 10128

99 98 97 96 95 5 4 3 2 1

Library of Congress Cataloging-in-Publication Data
Mitchison, Naomi, 1897-
Solution Three/ by Naomi Mitchison; afterword by Susan M. Squier.
Originally published: London: Dobson, 1975.
Includes bibliographical references (p.).
ISBN 1-55861-097-9: $29.95. -- ISBN 1-55861-096-0 (pbk.): $10.95
1. Human reproduction--Fiction. 2. Sexual orientation--Fiction.

I. Title.   PR6025.I86S57 1995

823'.912--dc20   94-32515
                                                  CIP

Cover design by Dennis Ascienzo
Solution Three was typeset by Bristol Typesetting Co., Ltd., Bristol,
England.
Printed in the United States of America on acid-free paper by
McNaughton & Gunn, Inc.

This publication is made possible, in part, by public funds from the
National Endowment for the Arts and the New York State Council on the
Arts. The Feminist Press would also like to thank Helene Goldfarb,
Joanne Markell, and Genevieve Vaughan for their generosity.

FOREWORD

The problems facing a writer of S.F. are somewhat the same
as those of a writer, either of historical fiction, or of stories
about people in another culture, with another language. In
the course of writing various books, I have had to consider all these rather similar problems of communication:
how to make things readable—I hope attractively readable—in one's own country or culture or historical epoch,
without losing the feeling of somewhere else. Clearly
Kleomenes, Vercingetorix or Cleopatra, did not speak
current English; but nothing would be gained by direct
translation from Greek or Gallic. The same thing holds
for, say, Hindu or Setswana, or even for Italian or Danish.
One only hopes to retain a flavour.

Clearly, if people a century or two centuries on—though
sometimes in S.F. one goes far further than this—speak
English, it will be very different from current English or
current American, perhaps more different than today's is
from Shakespeare's, which is about as far back as one can
go with complete ease, linguistically speaking, even when
one is aware that pronunciations and even the meanings of
some words, were not the same as today's. Again, what one
hopes for is a flavour, and here I have attempted to have
a slightly different flavour for two groups of clones: what,

5

in my own imagining, came easiest to their tongues. I have tried to pick this out, also, in the names of the girls and boys in the two groups.

From Shakespeare's time, words and phrases which were perhaps vulgar colloquialisms, have now come into respectable speech. I have almost certainly guessed wrong on what will survive from current slang. One chooses what one finds pleasing or amusing, oneself.

But there is something else. The interest of writing novels is to see what people will do in situations which one has invented for them. This seems to me to be supremely so in S.F. There are of course S.F. fans who are more interested in the details of the invented situations than in the people, and equally, there are S.F. writers who are better at handling the situation than the characters. I was brought up to biology rather than to physics; perhaps this shows through.

Two words that come into this book should be explained : —

1. A clone consists of the descendants of an individual produced through a-sexual reproduction, having identical genetic constitution.

2. Meiosis is a cell division in the germ cell line during the formation of eggs and sperm, which results in the chromosome number being halved and the genes re-assorted. Note that, when egg and sperm cells re-unite in the process of fertilization, one chromosome in a pair comes from each parent, so that the original number of chromosomes comes back, but there may be crossing over of chromosome material.

CHAPTER ONE

OVER the years the Council had met in several different places and many different ways. First, there had been the time of uncertainty, after the terrible crisis of Aggression and all that came of it, including the annihilation, as living and food-producing spaces, of large parts of the Earth's surface, including many major cities. Then the Councillors had kept to formality, sitting at spaced desks with the slight hum of the recording machines and the tiny clicks as they switched into their technical advisers and the picture beside the desk came alive and spoke. The first Council had been Her creation, Solution One, mainly to put through the food and population policy and to bring back sanity and order. Later, when it seemed as if things were working out, when they saw their idea of a world at last with a dropping population, and with a genuine diminution of aggression, group or personal, the Council had sat round a table which had flowers in the centre—real flowers to keep them in mind of values easily forgotten. They had even tried at one period, to work still more distantly by video-telephone, each in his or her own office or living space. That was at the time of Solution Two, but seemed not in accordance with the thoughts, either of Him or Her, and did not last long.

By that time He and She, as separate individuals, had both ceased; but the tissues which would continue them for ever, in all their excellence, were there to be used. True, the first attempts at continuance had been failures, but this too had been half expected. Human cloning had not yet been attempted though there had been mammalian cloning on a laboratory scale; nothing utterly new succeeds at once. As with so much scientific research, the direct approach often gave no results; one had to get at it, so to speak, from behind. The Professorials understood that; it was their glory. And then things had begun to go well, not only with cloning but with the world. By now the A to C Clones were all over twenty, their education finished, and their observation and participation beginning to show effect.

So at last, with Solution Three, there seemed to be the possibility of a peaceful humanity with problems which could at least be broken up into dimensions which the mind could grasp without discouragement, helped by the computers but not mastered by them: The Council were beginning to see results here and there. It was at this time that there was a continual discussion about the most appropriate meeting place. They had met at one time or another in all the continents, and even now an appropriate group would go back for business or formal discussions to some of the old places, the ravishingly lovely Council boat in Kashmir, or the strange clearing in the upper Amazon basin where the Council, through active participation, had succeeded in saving the culture of the last of the Amerindian tribes. The older cities had been so badly damaged during the Aggressions that even those which were again inhabitable were often crammed with bad memories and regrets. Thus it was thought sensible to have the main Council meetings in the new, completely planned mega-city of the northern temperate zone, where most of the cloning took place. There had, after all, to be careful watching and care for the Clones and the Clone Mums.

Some day, if all went well, it would be possible to break up the mega-cities into more varied and individual components, which the human mind could grasp and help. People on the whole would enjoy that, or so it was reported to the Council, yet many were curiously attached. And indeed this mega-city was in many ways very beautiful, built strictly for the purpose of saving the human population which was then necessarily crammed together, leaving as much land as possible for the food fields and, above all, equalizing the living space so that the old aggression provoking patterns were gone for ever.

In order to convince people that this was necessary and that they must make do with their living spaces, the buildings which held them were as beautiful as possible, with parks and play spaces wherever possible, often terraced up to a pleasant summit full of creepers rooting far below, so as to have no weight of earth to contend with. That was one reason why the mega-cities had to be completely new, uncontaminated by the old values, social or aesthetic. The younger post-aggression people, who had spent all their lives there, were really upset at the idea of something different and, to their minds, inconvenient; how could all the essential administrative and scientific centres be split up? Actually most of the astronomical and space work was done in another mega-city, and again, educational research and much public health came from a third. It was reasonably easy to communicate or even to travel personally. But the mega-city fans thought otherwise. You could talk all you liked about videophoning and instant all-language communication, but to make a new city, even with all the

A*

goodies of the freshest super-architecture and decoration, well, it wouldn't be the same as their very own safe old, dear old, mega-city.

So this was how it was that the first Council offices in the mega-city, dating from the desk days, had been over-planned with an impressive main hall so that everybody in the whole world could, if they chose, listen and see and participate in some meetings at least. But in settled times there was less and less interest. That was one of the problems: how to get participation without interest and how to get interest without having injustice or imbalance to put right? And the Council was having considerable success in eliminating these. Various ways of encouraging interest were tried out, not too successfully. Meanwhile the Council, or such members of it as were present, met more often and far less formally. In fact the old Council Chamber was now an air conditioned nursery for the Clones on the days when the out-door temperature control was not quite what it should be. The screens which used to show a technical adviser sitting at a Council-type desk, or flashed into sometimes angry life in the great days of participation for questions and answers from a world-wide, immediately translated audience, now showed entertainment and mild education. The Councillors met in a smaller room at the other end of the building. Not only did it have real flowers in the old tradition, but real water, even drinkable, and real fire. Fire and flowers reflected in water.

Behind Mutumba there was a ritualized picture, delicately painted perhaps in Bali or some other part of south east Asia. Hills rose, rivers meandered, angels or demons perched and flew. It was of course the historic meeting, Him and Her, both, as in real life, aged; but in the conventions of this picture, both were white haired, heavily wrinkled and haloed, and supported by followers in attitudes of devotion. Mutumba and the other Councillors knew well enough that the meeting had taken place in quite other, urban conditions, and that, considering their ages and what they had gone through, both looked unusually well preserved, a little impatient of help and in possession of all their faculties.

However, nobody paid much attention to the picture, although, with Mutumba as Convenor of the Council, they were bound to see it occasionally as they addressed her. But they had plenty of time : this was a much pleasanter place than their offices or laboratories or their living spaces, which were no larger or more comfortable than the norm, in fact less roomy than some. However, if a real population reduction was taking place, as appeared from the figures, plus an increasing percentage of Clones among the young people, either living space might become easier or, more probably, there would be more places of public or semi-public beauty, calm and absence of hurry and strain. Already the influence of the Clones was being felt, here and there, in the direction of that planning.

By now the main business was over; it had been hard and concentrated. Some had been about the difficulties in the way of acceptance of the code and population policy in parts of Africa and how it was being solved among the upper Amazon Amerindians who had been saved and studied with the utmost gentleness and withdrawal of pressures, but were now being lured into the world as it existed while keeping and even communicating the elements of their own very unusual happiness. There had been a report from a Council member, Diljit, himself of uncommon part-Indian ancestry, who had been with the Amerindians for many years. Clearly he had managed participation; although he wore an ordinary urban spray-on, he moved differently and his face showed different emotions from those of the other Council members. Yet he was communicating with them easily and all had found his data fascinating. Now he had left, to do some further recording and then go back. Although he was quite happy to see his old colleagues again, he had lost the habits of a mega-city and intended to head back as soon as possible for the Amazon.

There had been other matters. All the Council had been trained in statistical thinking, but knew it was not everything. Some had already left, to go back to urgent work or even urgent play, such as the probability games which involved large urban groups. The strict general attention of a good Council meeting had broken up into groups and movement.

Ric had been running through the statistics. His computer was designed and programmed to make them stylish, memorable and clear and to query doubtful figures. 'Any bother with your Mums?' he asked Jussie.

Jussie clipped two sheets together. 'Only the usual,' she said.

'Wanting a second go?' She nodded.

'You could well make the process of parturition less pleasant,' said Stig.

But Mutumba overhead. 'Don't you think that would be contrary to the Code?' she asked gently.

'Yes, Ma'am,' Stig muttered, using the formal designation because he felt a little ashamed.

Jussie leant across and picked up a sheet of Ric's statistics. 'There still seem to be a number of the Professorials giving birth. After actual copulation. Odd.' She sipped a glass of orange juice and curled into her chair. Once they had decided to give up their desks and screens and switches, they had opted for real comfort in their furnishings. They could stroll about, dip hands or feet in the running water, pick the real flowers, or leave the room to consult books or maps or other information sources or memory banks. This was part of the Code, Her doing mostly. They were by no means all there; as usual, some were away on missions or just listening in to what was happening anywhere and everywhere; some, like Diljit, had been away for years. Others, on shorter assignments, had reported and been questioned, sometimes under memory recalling drugs when they had been in situations where note taking or minimal recording was impossible. The processes of the Council were continuous.

'Do we go on with the Professorials? Letting them behave in these unsocial ways?' said Stig to nobody in particular. 'To me, they smell bad.' He seemed to be in a wretched mood. Hiji moved nearer to him and put his small, brown palm onto Stig's knee. The mood would pass. The other Councillors knew quite well this feeling against the Professorials. All of them had experienced it from time to time and got over it. There was a fairly small percentage of the population who had not moved to what was now called Solution Three. Too bad for them. But the number was statistically small. Let it pass.

'We all realize right-on that they are social misfits,' said Mutumba. 'Something just hasn't taken. We're in process of finding out why and what. But for certain important purposes they are needed and must be allowed their compensations. Such as they apparently are. Without superiority feelings. You know that as well as I do, Stig. It's in the Code.'

And one or two of them murmured, 'The Code.'

'Now, friends,' said Mutumba, suddenly brisk and fully

herself, 'I think we're through. Right? Anyway with the main business, and now this cat is stepping down. But no hurry. No hurry at all. Take your time. We can resume if we need to.' She bent over the flowers and took a big sniff. She was broad nostrilled, broad hipped, a glowing brown, and the spray-on dress she was wearing had beautifully multi-coloured folds; but her close hair was almost white; no Councillor would have altered this token of seniority. Looking over to blue-eyed, frowning Stig, she remembered her own difficult clone birth and the enchantment of her blue-eyed white baby, for her Clone had been from Her. And She, of course, was White like the other Shetlanders. Shetland, yes, they had taken her there for pre-natal authenticity, what a place to come from! The cliffs and the sea and the oil ruins, that decade of mad prosperity, gone.

Jussie was saying to Ric: 'I have the same feeling sometimes. I suppose it's just that I find the Professorials difficult to understand.'

'You mean their hetero-sexuality?' Ric said it bravely, for it was really rather an unpleasant word.

Jussie nodded. 'You see, it means—oh dear, not so much the men, perhaps, but a woman actually admiring, touching, being touched by—so disordered!'

'It happened in history,' said Ric soberly, 'and not so far back either, before Solution Three, the great step in human self-knowledge and control.' But why be so pompous! 'You must have read about it.'

'I hate reading about it—these dreadful external sex organs!' said Jussie, and then, 'Oh Ric, I do apologize, I never think of you as a male, but I suppose you're bound to have them.'

'I know, I know,' said Ric soothingly, 'but there are bits of you that flop, Jussie, if you don't mind my saying so.'

She did, but then she realized how tired they both were after the meeting. The basic thirty hour week didn't mean a thing to Councillors, they just had to go on. They looked at one another and laughed.

Jussie leant over and patted Ric. 'Well, anyhow there go the poor old Professorials doing their thing which it seems they can't help doing, but producing technology for the rest of us.'

'Lovely, lovely technology!' sang out Elissa, coming over to them with a couple of the film capsules she had been demonstrating earlier, and smiling at Jussie, showing off her own debt to technology. She was always happening on a new sprayer; not being one for folds and swirls, she had taken a close off-crimson spray that ended in fine lines whiskering out a few centimetres from her golden ears, the same down toewards from her ankles. This had been topped off with wavy lines reminding the viewer of—what? Ric found her just a little repulsive, as after all, women normally were, though this was easily blotted out with a colleague, Mutumba or Jussie or Shanti. But as she came near, Jussie looked hungrily and simply had to stroke Elissa down, a long shoulder to buttocks, and pull her for a moment into the same chair. Elissa responded with a quick hand between Jussie's legs, but just as a greeting. Really, she had hoped that Mutumba would notice her, but Mutumba was talking to Stig and Andrei and only smiled briefly and in an un-lit-up way at Elissa who was, all the same, one of the brightest of the younger Councillors and had produced some exceedingly good ideas while business was on. And was about to go off on a dangerous mission.

And not so long ago, thought Ric, as history time goes, Elissa would doubtless have thrown herself at me, yes, me! Oh, with legs and arms open, those breasts pointing like greedy animals and I would have responded and scrambled under her—no, over—and got into her, how revolting, and she would have sucked me in and held me—no, I can't think of it! He looked for relief at gentle, slender, narrow should-ered Hiji all in black but for his silver badge. Yes, it had been like that, and the women giving birth, popping the new lives out, over-populating, until at last it was realized that attraction between the sexes was only a snare and an aggression; the real thing was man to man and woman to woman. There alone was love. Ric believed deeply in love; it was strength; it was part of the Code. But, in the old inter-sex pattern, it had always led to violence and pain. Students of historical literature, as he had been, understood this well. Tragedy, tragedy. Shakespeare, Molière, Tolstoy, the lot, right up to the great break-through.

One saw these tragedies re-enacted among the Profes-sorials and other dissenters. They agreed with the code in principle. How not? In fact the Cloning was due to Pro-fessorials. It could never have been done without the work of the biologists Quereshi and the great Sen and, earlier, Watson and Mitchison. But the Professorials had been un-willing to accept the inevitable new morality of Solution Three, essential to human survival, and, according to the code, force was not to be used on them. Only understand-ing. Some of them, naturally, had come into a state of agree-ment and even enthusiasm, but the majority of the non-clone births were among this class. There were still, no doubt, quite a few elsewhere, but the absolute numbers dropped year by year. People do not on the whole break their customs and social morality and face the disapproval of their peer group for something as unimportant as inter-sexual love.

There had of course been some intensive school-age

hormone and psychological treatment during the years of population crisis. It could be laid on more subtly now if there seemed to be a relaxing of social imperatives in any group. The children of inter-sex marriages were carefully watched and, if necessary, treated. All this was one of the important monitoring jobs for the members of the Council who were away on their duties all about the world. There might, for instance, be a recrudescence in India, or, more rarely, Africa, usually associated with some religious revival. So far, all had been contained.

And there was Ric's colleague and friend Jussie, approaching Elissa. Really, really! Though of course in a way highly suitable. Nothing to be shocked at, only Ric just couldn't imagine the attraction. After a little they appeared hand in hand and Jussie was gently pulling Elissa towards the sauna room. And they would roll around on the floor no doubt and take the birch twigs to one another and tickle up one another's nipples and those other parts which he had been shown as video-tactiles in his adolescence, made to touch, and found as revolting as half decayed meat. Well, well, if they enjoyed it, perhaps one should think no more about it. It was all right and proper. Jussie was a splendid worker and colleague; she was no longer young; she had many friends, but no one, he thought, special. Yes, it was fortunate that Elissa had allowed herself to be attracted. Yes, Jussie deserved every bit of happiness she could get.

Yet how different it seemed from love as he knew it. Hiji. And then the young Bobbi, the Clone boy, the existing, moving sliver of Him, eighteen years old, already intent on the purpose which those genes revealed to him. Could he, Ric, unworthy, trying to make a better world but failing so often, could he ever allow the deep love he felt to turn

17

into words? Into a poem which Bobbi might read? Or should the Clone boys love only one another, heightening and strengthening their powers for good? And the Clone girls from Her the same? If they must: if *that* could be love. Yet was not he, wrongly, feeling a revulsion against the other sex, even the Clone girls? Oh wrong, wrong, wrong. To hate or despise the other sex, not because it interfered with him or threatened him, but for itself? He was in danger of transgressing the code. He must go and talk with the Convenor. She would care for him. She would show him where he had slipped and set him right again.

CHAPTER TWO

JUSSIE was feeling her living-space somehow closing in on her. When Elissa was there it had seemed just right, an elegant box, sized for two to be very near in. But Elissa was away and might or might not come back; she had to monitor an area of her native continent. There had been trouble, flags and shouting, things said that should not be said. News of a few murders had already come in. If the leaders of this local difficulty were to recognize her, as they well might—well, all Councillors faced danger sooner or later. Jussie remembered one or two incidents in her own life, when she had been horribly frightened. Oh, years and years ago when she herself was a young Councillor. But the Code had strengthened her : she had kept her head. It had turned out all right in the end. When one thought of the dangers He had faced. Yes. Both of Them.

There was not much in the living space to like; she had preferred to keep it reasonably empty, though there was the usual *toko-no-ma* niche for an art object, which she did not always bother to change daily or even weekly. So many pictures and toys and objects of convenience or amusement could be found in the public buildings, for that matter in the Council rooms themselves, that one didn't want them staring at one. She had not fussed, just taken the living space which had been allotted to her, years ago now; it would have been very bad form for a Councillor to do otherwise. But it would have been nice to have an outside window. The viewing screen could of course show her all the world, forests and deserts, or a perpetual heave and foaming of lonely waves; she could either have sound or leave it, the same with the still rather unsatisfactory scent programme which, in fact, she never bothered with. One could have art programmes, choosing a museum or gallery, stopping it at a chosen point. But—well, but. She could smell Elissa on the cushions and in the bathroom. For a little she switched to Elissa's continent, the sprawling, only half-planned cities, where the picture shifted from an occasional gorgeous building to a street of mean little houses, although there were always the planned areas with decent living spaces, doubtless air-conditioned and with power supplies, into which people were being shifted. Anywhere near the sea and you saw the great desalination works for the water supplies. There were recreation spaces being laid out and planted. Schools. Children. Surplus population, though not unattractive in their way. But not nearly so many of these as there would have been in a picture taken thirty years back, still less than there would surely have been a century and more ago, in the days of the population crisis. Then across fields rich with the new types of maize and rice and wheat, men and women busy on still un-automated irrigation, and then, suddenly, onto still unaltered forest, occasionally even, some quick, low beast moving between branches. Would Elissa get into one of these wild spaces, or would she have to be in the cities all the time? Elissa with all the grace of a wild creature. Elissa.

She turned the picture back to the fields, trying to get a close look, presumably from a low-flying plane. Was that wheat field a bit uneven? Hard to be sure. There had been various worries lately, rather new diseases affecting the standard hybrids. It might be the fertilizers, and yet these had all been carefully and lengthily checked. Experimental work was being done, in an attempt to find immune varieties which would have the same high yields and easy harvesting peculiarities. So far results had been uncomfortably negative. It now began to seem probable that in the course of breeding, some of the genes had been knocked out, ones with unwanted characteristics, but also perhaps carrying guards against certain funguses, bacteria or viruses, which might now have found their way through.

It was not so easy to go back and replace a gene even if one could make the inspired guess as to which it was. And it was likely that, for example, the viruses which had originally been guarded against might have altered in all kinds of subtle and largely invisible ways. Viruses were still awkward little devils. But that kind of biological inspiration was something that some of the Professorials had developed and it was to be hoped that it might happen once more. The gene or genes would have to be found again, to start with, but so many of the early varieties of wheat, maize, sorghum and the rest, had simply disappeared. Everyone, almost everywhere, grew the new ones. The same thing had happened with the leguminous crops, beans and lentils, though so far no new diseases threatened them. Elissa, on her essentially social and political mission would also look out for the occasional backward area where some deeply ignorant farmer was still growing the old corn. And perhaps producing surplus population into the bargain. Famine was still a threat to Mother earth, but hiding round another corner to be outwitted another way.

She wondered how the wheat programme was doing.

They'd had no reports from the Professorials for some time. Perhaps she would screen up Miryam and ask. Would she be in the lab now? Or in her living space? Was it evening yet? How nicely an outside window gave one an idea of time passing! But she mustn't think that, very rarely did think it, only when troubled. Jussie looked at her watch; Elissa's jet would be almost there now. And how would the airport be? A very possible trouble spot. But Elissa had gone off in tearing spirits! Yes, Miryam would be bound to be back in her living space. Jussie screened through, giving her identity and asking for admission. Well, Miryam seemed pleased to see her! But her living space was more cluttered than ever. A child had been building something, and clearly Miryam had just shooed him off. Fair enough. One didn't obtrude such things.

They had an interesting discussion. Miryam had been trying out one of the old Andean maizes which had been discovered beside a village which was long deserted, half buried in volcanic ash. But a few plants had survived, sheltered by a large rock. It had been a great piece of luck. They went on to wheats, but Miryam kept looking over her shoulder, obviously distressed. 'One moment!' she said, and blacked out. When she came back on she started apologizing. Jussie noticed that the child's construction had fallen over.

But Jussie made soothing remarks. Miryam mustn't be frightened; that wasn't what the Council was for, nobody was interfering. Of course Jussie knew that Miryam had a hetero-sexual relation and a child—no, two—as a result. No doubt poor Miryam found it painful and embarrassing, which was no reason for anyone else to refer to it. The computers knew, of course, but there was no reason to consult them as between people who respected one another. If she decided to end the relation—or if he did, and naturally Jussie knew who he was and whose colleague he would be, since he was working on cell structure while she was a plant geneticist—that would be fine. Both would certainly re-make a happier and more suitable love relation.

And the children? They would go to their lovely schools, which now had rather small classes, and if there was any slight tendency—and naturally children were apt to be imprinted by early experiences—it could be corrected by the child watchers. And by the Clone children themselves, some of whom would be at the same schools, Him and Her forever multiplied, whose instincts would not need watching. Poor Miryam, caught in this sad old social pattern, who might have been so happy and normal and was indeed quite attractive! Jussie herself always felt warmly towards Miryam and would have liked to help her. Perhaps one day she would be able to do just that.

The Professorials had been so much harder to deal with than the lower IQ's, bless their hearts. With them, social changes could be made through the ordinary advertisement channels, once one got hold of them. Persuasion was, after all, such an expert business; it had only to be applied, both subliminally and overtly, through the many media. The essential was to get at the females and so much more could be done through a slanting of their favourite reading. But the Professorials tended to like literature of the kind which was fixed and could not be slanted, although much critical work was being done on Shakespeare, Dante, the Kama Sutra and in fact all the classics. There had also been a build-up of the already appropriate authors, from Plato to Proust, Gide, Cavafy, Forster and many others. The excitement of finding the hidden Leonardo note-book!

However, as the persuaders increased the slant in popular

reading, it all snowballed. Men, after all, had always had their best and noblest relations with one another. So, naturally, had women. Here it was merely a case of lifting the shadow from them—the thoughts of the old people, the earth shadow; then they shone out. But there had been this reluctance among the Professorials, partly because they were less open to the persuaders and their media and partly through a curious tradition of opposition. Yes, opposition to any government, even in the face of the plainest social danger. Opposition to Him and Her.

But it had been nice for Jussie, talking to Miryam, and reassuring that the geneticists had got onto the Andean strain. There were probably still wild wheats, triticums of some kind, in parts of central Asia, small places which had resisted education. Yes, just as the Professorials had! People for whom He was Lenin or Mao and She was the Virgin— unfortunately the Virgin Mother. Or possibly Kwan Yin. Well, at some stages of development a lot of mix-up was inevitable. One should not complain, so long as it did not lead to aggression.

Jussie began to walk about her living space, seven paces by six and so much taken up by the big screen, the video, the tape runner with the viewers and so on, not to speak of the small alcove with the heat ray and disposer. She began to alter the shapes and colours of the chairs and couch, moulding and pulling the material, twisting the crystals of the colour-mix. It did no good. If Elissa was to come back suddenly—no. She wished she cared more for music; but her own genes had been wrong for that. What would it be like, she thought to herself, to be actually one of the Clones, the rising forest of genetic excellence? Well, she would go over and see how the Clone Mums were doing. She moved to the fast lift, then into the tunnel and the moving platform of the walkway. She was pleased to see that a new mural was being thrown onto the walls, sea bottom with rocks and live corals, swaying weeds and swimming or darting fish. Very pleasant, though one might get to know it too well. She had been bored with the old mountain landscape, all those waterfalls. They should be changed more often : ideally, every day. But that, like many other things, would have to wait. First things first.

It was good, too, to note how few children one now saw on the walkways, though there were plenty of vigorous, cheerful young people. Or at least they looked young; one did when one led an interesting life with creative play and of course modern health techniques. And none of the old basic anxieties and insecurities. Some might look young, all the same, but perhaps dated from the immediate post-aggression years as she herself did. What one had seen and done in a lifetime! And as she thought of it, she came to the gardens, making her way in through one of the side entrances. She took a deep breath. There was nothing wrong with the air that came into her living space or, for that matter, in the tunnel, but somehow it did not please nostrils or lungs as this did.

The gardens were full of babies and toddlers, white females and dark brown males. Although it was under an open sky, at which Jussie looked up happily, before even noticing the babies, there was a subtle ground temperature adjustment, so that the little ones needed only to wear the lightest of tiny spray-ons or nothing at all, according to the pleasure of the Mums. As the babies tended to congregate as soon as they were old enough to be mobile, and this was unusually early, the Mums did the same. There was plenty of room. And how delightful that was, both for Jussie and the Mums. After the living spaces and offices or the unfortunately still crowded recreation or holiday spaces, how wonderful for each human being was the mere fact of being able to see as far as unimpeded sky or, uninterruptedly, as far as some little lake or island or flowering bush that seemed to be waiting, to be existing, for oneself alone! The living space blocks which had garden tops were a little unsatisfactory: it seemed to be a human body-need to have, sometimes, earth underfoot and sky overhead: primitive perhaps, but a fact for the sociologists to recognize. The world held also, of course, the wild spaces, mountain tops and some remaining forest and desert areas, but they were not easy to get at. Few people bothered to go there, though Jussie herself had been to the Antarctic penguin land, taking time off from professional service in the mines, and had also once been in the Himalayas, a high remote valley, too far for food growing. It remained in the back of her mind. Happily? In a way.

She walked on. There were two Mums lying on a grass bank half under the trailing branches of a cherry in flower. The seasons here had been genetically jumbled, so that the strangest combinations of flowers and fruit coincided. It always took the Mums a little while to dare, to get used to actually walking on the genuine, living grass. Almost all went barefoot, and this was encouraged. It was certain that His Mum had gone barefoot, possible that Her's had in summer, the short northern summer on the rare sand beaches or the close turf of the scattald. It was obligatory to read what was known about Him and Her, and especially their Mums. Just possibly a certain copying of the pattern might have some result on the foetus; one could not, as yet, give a definite yes or no answer.

Jussie watched them from a little distance, smiling, for it was a pretty play and they were too engrossed to notice.

Which were they?—oh, Allie and Burd, both in their last month. They wore the lightest of loose spray-ons and both had clearly been to the amusement sector where it was made so easy, with only the smallest degree of luck or skill, to win necklaces, bracelets and anklets, flimsy as flowers but delightful for a day, and to have oneself or one's friend scented or shaved or powdered excitingly. The splendid mounds of their pregnancies were trailed over by cherry blossoms. Allie was fascinatedly caressing Burd's great smooth curve, while Burd was busy with Allie's buttocks, which were also putting on weight. All four breasts looked promising for the next stage. Burd began to tip Allie's with petals, then shook down a few, ticklingly, into a lower level. The game became more intimate, the great mounds heaved with pleasure.

Jussie left them to it while she went to look at a group of babies, all so admirably alike, then came back, with a word on her way for some of the watchers and carers. Allie and Burd were now quiescent, sweating, their eyes half shut, their fingers twined. 'Well,' said Jussie, 'happy? Any worries? Just tell me anything. I'm here to help.'

Allie propped herself up and giggled a little, shaking her head to get her own and Burd's hair out of her mouth. 'We couldn't be doing any harm, could we, to—to Them?'

'By what you were up to? Of course not. It was only natural and right. You're doing your pre-natal exercises as well, aren't you? Yes, that's splendid. Enjoy yourselves. There are going to be fireworks tonight. They'll look lovely among the fountains.'

She went on. How wonderful to have these young things to look after. So many in the main rush of the sex-tide, discovering one another's delicious possibilities and uses. And most were quite ordinary young women, chosen on physical

27

standards only; the genetic background made no difference. Both these two were a racial mixture, though Allie was very blonde and heavy, not at all her own type, but clearly Burd's. Burd was going to have a black boy, Allie a white girl. The I.Q. made little difference so long as there was a reasonable degree of responsibility, enough to understand and accept the instructions and suggestions and to read the books. The first Clone Mums had been high I.Q.'s, very responsible, very much aware, people like Mutumba and splendid Lisa, Andrei's elder sister, who had been murdered by the Mormons in the bad year. At first, too, there had been certain risks and dangers which had now been ironed out. Jussie herself had been too deeply involved, first as a mining engineer and then in Council work during the years when she might have been a Mum, and perhaps for that matter, it was not really her thing.

In a further part of the garden she found some of the slightly older children with all their admirable play things, designed to waken and increase their capacities, and also to make it easier to spot and evaluate their Signs, when they appeared. Much thought and experimental work had gone into this. Watching the children, it was clear that, even before they could talk, they were recognizing one another, making friends and little permanent groups, communicating. How could they recognize one another? There must be tiny differences, only perceptible to the other children. The Mums could find them by their ankle tags if necessary, but each child naturally knew its own Mum, so affection was continuous and guaranteed. 'No Signs yet, Gisela?' asked Jussie of one of the Mums, a soft, curly blonde, who was bouncing a ball invitingly for her own laughing little Clone, his mouth soft red in the deep brown of his skin, his milk-teeth white and even.

'Oh no!' said Gisela, with big, earnest eyes, 'you know I'd say the very minute—'

'Yes, I do know. I can trust you, Gisela. F Seventy One is very precious, very wonderful. And your doing.'

Yes, for the moment every Clone Mum was a person of deep importance. It would only last for a little while, but would colour the rest of their lives, whatever happened to them. And probably not much would happen. They would do work which interested and satisfied them, among friends, without too much painful responsibility or major choices. They would play games, love. Two Mums whose relationship in the gardens had been specially close, like Allie and Burd, would continue it later; they would feel themselves special, remembering and re-creating that atmosphere. Had golden-haired Gisela a special friend, Jussie wondered for a moment. Yes, Gisela had just that.

CHAPTER THREE

THE Clone Mums were all colours, many nationalities; the mega-cities had welcomed everyone equally; it was in the Code. But the baby boys were all brown, just as the baby girls were all white or rather, rose-pink. The baby boys had fuzzy, curly hair all alike. All alike except, thought Gisela, that Lilac had managed to brush her Ninety's hair into a sweet little crest. Should she have done that, even if it was so lovely, playing with their skin and hair, knowing that they were—Him? But Lilac was such fun, so sensible, so educated, so admired, so—yes, so loved. Why shouldn't she? F Ninety and F Seventy One were building with fitting blocks, jabbering gently and unintelligibly to one another, sometimes pushing away one of the others. One could see the Signs sometimes when children started construction; she knew that. So, of course, did Lilac.

They were sitting together, in the space and quiet. Gisela and Lilac. Together always. There was a lilac bush close to them, the great purple, damp-scented heads, full out. Lilac had been named for a favourite poem out of the old, old days: 'When lilacs last in the door-yard bloomed.' She could just remember her Dad quoting it, waving his arms as though he'd been hurt. For there were no lilacs. No door-yards. She hadn't liked the lilacs they had given her on her

birthday, the best art-blooms, scent guaranteed like real.
In some sense she couldn't quite say it wasn't the same
as this one that she could plunge her face into : this live
lilac scent which was a little symphonic, since part of it
came from the opening buds and part from slightly faded
flowerets, with perhaps a background of leaves and bark.
It was a tree the birds liked, these charming birds that used
the gardens, probably never moving out, since the mega-
city surrounded them, and very tame because their favourite
flowers were grown for them, scarlet creepers for the sun
birds on partly heated walls, but northern berries for black-
birds and pine cones for crossbills, and also because they
knew that nobody would harm them. By now Lilac could
tell them by their song, comparing it with the records;
Gisela loved being told, loved all these new names.

Some parts of the gardens had music, some, blessedly,
had nothing. Plane paths were deflected away from the
gardens, though at night the many communication satel-
lites made a friendly bobbing in and out of the old constel-
lations. There were plenty of amusements. The Mums could
video to friends as much as they liked. And there was the
splendid central building, dating back, in part, to the almost
remote past, incorporating, among other objects of interest
and education, a cathedral in which sounds, smells, everything, was authentic, and two terrifying tenements with
life-like occupants, one of which had come from Calcutta,
the other from Monte Video. But it had also music and
books and the scanners that went with them, pictures, mul-
tiple screening and ample leisure and play space in un-
favourable weather. 'Poor thing, she looks ever so tired,'
said Lilac, her eyes following Jussie out. 'I kind of like her,
better than the other cats.'

'It must be a terrible responsibility being a Councillor,'

said Gisela. 'Not even a thirty hour week! No wonder her hair isn't quite—you know. And that dress. It doesn't look as if she had anyone to dress for.'

Lilac shifted slightly, half-turning towards Gisela. Her own spray-on, clinging here and swinging there, was transparent wherever it mattered. Clone Mums were carefully readjusted after parturition to cosmetic perfection. 'I wouldn't be one of them, not for anything,' Lilac said, 'not just the hard work, but—well, they're bits of the machine. Them, I call it. So are the watchers and carers.'

'I don't see,' said Gisela, 'tell me, Lilac. Tell me about Them.' It was lovely having Lilac to tell her things. And the Clone babies were toddling and crawling for more bricks. Were they matching colours? No, not quite.

'Well, you know the library. It wouldn't be there if they didn't want us to read—would it?'

'I suppose not. But I can't be bothered with putting film through. Except about Him. Pictures are best. I like the pictures of Her Mum, teaching in that funny little school on the island. And outside seagulls and grass and little flowers. And ever so dark in winter!'

'But pictures don't always explain. Look, I've been reading history. You've no idea, Gisela.' No, Gisela had no idea. 'It's about police states: power and police. Where people don't matter. They were all over.'

'But He stopped them. I know that. First in America where all those awful things got done to Him, ooh I couldn't look! And there were the Aggressions. Then, once one of those big States went, they all went and what people were afraid of didn't happen.'

'Yes, that's right. The world was able to go on. And She'd been getting at it differently. But listen! You and I are being fed into a machine, just like people used to be. No, not just like. Nicely. Kindly. Nobody'd ever do the things to us they did to Him.'

'Only they had to happen, to strengthen Him,' murmured Gisela.

'Yes, yes, I know. But look, Gisela, we're all just doing what the Council plan. The Council—that's Them. They've got it all laid out. You know, the policies. The Code. What they call Solution Three. We aren't asked.'

'But should we be? I wouldn't know what to think.'

'Yes, we should. People used to come to Council meetings but they don't much now, even when they're specially asked; they let the Council go ahead with anything. Even the news-casts. None of us can be bothered to look at them unless it's something very special.'

Gisela went over and gently separated the two baby boys who were poking interestedly at one another's eyes. She started up one of the runabout toys and then came back to Lilac: 'Well, what would be the good of having a Council and all the people like poor Jussie working so hard, if we'd got to do it too? Wouldn't a Council meeting be ever so boring to watch? When they put them on the news-casts I always switch off. Don't you?'

'But that's it. We've let it happen. We've had the policies explained but they're difficult and there's so much else to do. I mean—well, for instance, there are the big skill games that everyone joins in and the painting and making halls, and the recreation areas—'

'I like making fountains do my thing—'

'Yes, you naughty!' It was Gisela's gayest accomplishment. 'But it's nothing to do with the policy. No, Gisela, listen. We know the policies have got aggression right out and that was what really mattered. And we know the popu-curve is going down and there's going to be more room.

There'll be gardens like this, not just for special people like us, but for everyone. Only—'

'Well then, why should we bother, my lovely?' Gisela's fingers were beginning to want to explore again, again.

'We ought to be asking questions. We know all the good things, but suppose there were bad things too? Oughtn't we to find out?'

'Oh you are silly, Lilac. You're reading too many of these old books, that's all it is! Yes, I know they're there, but we don't have to read them. Look, I do believe my Seventy One is matching colours! That—that's almost—oh could it be—!'

'No, he isn't. He isn't. Neither of them is.'

'I suppose not. But aren't they darling?'

For a moment both of them watched, loving, loving. One of the small, sleek, softly padding felines wove its way between the Clone babies, tickling them, and then sprang out of reach. Experience of contact.

'Big questions,' Lilac went on, 'right from the very bottom before the policies. Oh Gisela, we don't know what it was like. Some things were dreadful. All this aggression, people thinking of nothing except how to kill other people. Everything nice getting broken, all over the world. And then— smaller things. I found out, for instance, that in the old days, boys and girls had to do what they called exams. It was a kind of sudden stress put on. They died sometimes. Killed themselves.'

'Oh, Lilac, the things you do find out! But was it some sort of—strengthening? But for anyone. Unworthy people, so they couldn't take it?'

'Perhaps. It was wrong anyway. But the old days were ever so different. Things people did. You know men and women used to—'

34

But Gisela covered her ears: 'You haven't been having thoughts, Lilac, oh no!' How could Lilac, her beloved, say such things! Gisela began to kiss, felt her tense but softening. 'You're joking, Lilac! You don't want to be like one of those poor Professorials!'

'No, not exactly. But—something doesn't seem quite right. That's what I mean about Them, and about us being only part of a plan. I keep thinking. Even here, even with our lovely, lovely babies, even with you, my little sweetie.'

Not quite right? What was getting at Lilac? Not quite right, here in the gardens, the nicest place in the world, these real flowers, these butterflies—oh look at that one!— specially brought from all the world over and bred here, and the small tame creatures, the squirrels and small deer and koala bears, all for them, the chosen, the Clone Mums, them and their little ones! And suddenly she said: 'Lilac, you've made Ninety's hair look different from the others. Ought you to?'

Astonishingly, Lilac answered with a giggle: 'Why not? He's mine.'

But of course, he wasn't. That was the whole point and naturally, Lilac knew it as well as anyone. The Clones didn't belong to the Mums who had been their nests and love givers, but whose own cell nucleus had been eliminated at an early stage. If anything it was the other way, the Mums belonging to the Clones, for little children must have love until—until the moment when the Signs showed that babyhood had ended, that here again were He and She, and then the period of strengthening when, in a time-shortened psychological copy of the stresses in His and Her life, they were taken away and things were made to happen to them. At first, as was well known, this had been done in adoles-

35

cence, but there had been two or three disastrous results. Better that it should happen in childhood when the impact could be built onto later as the personality stabilized. Hence the watching for the Signs which would show that the time had come. The Mums were told all this carefully and truthfully, though the details of the toughening process were not usually referred to. It was also explained that in the earliest years the Mums never saw their Clones again and were not allowed to get in touch.

That had been still more severe at the beginning. Mutumba herself had no idea what had happened to her little flax haired Clone, whom she had cried for secretly and long. Nor did she try to find out; a Councillor must not break the code. But today Mums were allowed a limited contact later on; a few were even allowed the privilege of choosing their Clone's name when he or she ceased to be a number.

And now Lilac had said this dreadful thing and with the special smile that brought Gisela struggling after her like a hooked fish. 'But they aren't ours!' Gisela cried, 'and you know it!'

'Oh, I know they aren't ours genetically,' Lilac said and then, in a lower voice : 'Of course I knew all about it before I became a Mum; nothing was kept from me. But all the same once he was there, inside me, I felt angry, cheated. I wanted him to be partly me. Oh yes, yes, we aren't worthy and all that. They're only lent to us. But that's how I felt. Didn't you ever, Gisela, lovey, didn't you, didn't you?'

Gisela half pulled away : 'If I had—if I'd found these wrong thoughts in me—but I wouldn't have let myself— I'd have gone to my own carer, she'd have put me right! Oh please, Lilac, let's go, let's find your special carer! That's Darya, isn't it?'

'No,' said Lilac, and lay down along the bench with her head in Gisela's lap, looking up at her, 'No.'

So what was poor Gisela to do? Speak to one of the watchers? Oh no, impossible! So what? Nothing. Let it pass. Forget, yes, yes, forget, it hadn't happened. They'd see the Signs soon and then—well then, they'd go back to the real world. Only she and Lilac would go on and on, for ever and ever! Loving, loving, the only thing that matters. There, now Lilac had shut her eyes, she was forgetting it too. Her long dark eyelashes. She hadn't really said any of those things.

Gisela was beginning to wonder about going back. Darling Seventy One was so nearly showing the Signs. Oh how proud of him she'd be. And then, there'd be the ceremony and after that yes, she'd like to see her own Mum again. She was an operator in one of the big spray-ons. Did design too. She'd been so proud of Gisela being chosen and told everyone!

Her Dad had gone off to one of the men's colonies; he was proud of her too. Sometimes he used to pay a visit, but it wasn't embarrassing, he never looked nasty. After all, thirty years ago a lot of ordinary people hadn't really known, not like everyone knew now, so you couldn't blame them. So that was all right and she'd like to meet her Dad again. There'd be a celebration, maybe they'd even go on one of the space platforms, oh she'd like that! It was special privilege, she knew, but after all she'd been a Clone Mum. What was more, everyone would know; if once you'd been a Clone Mum you were looked up to. Girls you never thought you'd get to know would come up and ask you about it.

Seventy One and Ninety were pushing their fingers through slits in the toy they had hold of. And to think that they truly were—Him. Wasn't it wonderful, being His

37

Mum. You wouldn't want to mix your own poor little self up with it. Lilac couldn't have wanted that, not really. Gisela began again thinking about going back. A Clone Mum could go free into all the recreation and game-play spaces and yes, she'd like to have a go on the real razzle-dazzle-rips again! Everyone screaming and holding on like mad. You got amusements in the gardens, but only quiet ones. Even the fireworks were only lights and rockets, not big bangs that made everyone jump. At first she'd thought she'd never want to leave. But it was like they'd all said: three years was enough. If only she and Lilac could see the Signs at the same time and have the ceremony and leave together! It might be any time now, when the babies got to proper construction, not just fitting the blocks together anyhow, but having a purpose. She'd seen so many screenings, she was sure she'd spot it.

And suddenly she had a dreadful idea and leant close, whispering into the silky red-brown hair spread over her lap: 'Lilac, wake up! Lilac, my darling, my own, ownest darling, you haven't—you haven't seen the Signs and not told?' But Lilac opened her eyes and looked straight up into her face. And Lilac only smiled.

CHAPTER FOUR

MIRYAM closed the video circuit so that she could not be called up. She changed the art object in the alcove of the *toko-no-ma*. Then she curtained off the cot and the small bed; but if only there was more room! Lu was asleep, with his hand still clutched onto a toy. But Little Em was fidgeting away, half awake, her eyelids fighting with sleep, her mouth making half sucking movements against the blanket. Little Em. I think I would break my heart if she ever wants to be a Clone Mum. Instead of a real one. And yet that's just what may happen. We don't know what the policy will be over the next twenty years. A pity they don't trust us more. If they succeeded— And yet in so many ways they are right; it was perhaps the only policy at the time: riding the wave: solution three. When nothing else stopped the population rise: contraceptives, abortion, rising standard of living. All failing: only this way could have worked. Or so we think now. No, Em, my little love, sleep, sleep.

Tiptoeing back from the curtain, Miryam looked down at her well shaped legs, rather conservatively sprayed, but it was the colour he most liked, or rather the combination of colours, though that was something he never quite understood! That day they first decided. Thinking back to it, Miryam waited for the discreet door touch; then she was in his arms and everything—wanting more room, what might happen to Little Em, work problems—suddenly became curiously bearable. She dimmed the light and they sat down, but Carlo's long legs almost reached the picture screen. Then a pile of books came tumbling down. Luckily she had very few books, though thousands of the tiny cassettes that she ordinarily used for video-audio. But the children were soundly off now. She and Carlo were both good scientists, not quite top flight perhaps, but if they had been living normal lives with their own kind, she knew that things would have been made easier. As it was, she was always being missed out when bigger living spaces were allocated; so was he.

Instead of being normal they were married. Yes, it was still possible, though difficulties were put in their way; there were various checks and humiliations and delays. But actual monogamous marriage was usually feasible for the Professorials at least. They had a few friends in the same state, which was comforting. From time to time they could visit one another and get a little strength and confidence and laughter. But these marriages did not always work. If once either of the partners began to feel guilty, the social structure of their tiny minority seemed to melt away. And how to avoid guilt with their colleague's eyes and tongues on them? Miryam and Carlo searched themselves for guilt and often enough one or the other of them had felt it when they were in normal company. But ordinarily, being together wiped it out.

Carlo had brought a nice looking packet with some fancy name—leaf protein or algal protein to start with no doubt! But the taste-cookies had done a good job. You wouldn't know it from real. As he turned the instant ray onto it, the smell wafted onto their taste buds. Cleverly, the disposable plates remained cool enough to touch. Miryam sat on Carlo's knee, which was practical considering the space, and gave them a chance of feeding one another tid-bits. Oh dear, she did seem to have rather a lot of papers and reference cassettes, even with so many at the lab, and she had to have somewhere for Lu's toys! Little Em was only just starting to play, so she didn't need so many; and besides, they would soon be following the child's code of sharing; the day nursery would see to that, though she would follow up at home.

She was lucky that there was still a day nursery at the lab, with a couple of old ladies in charge, too old to disapprove: the lab babies had been much approved of in their young days before the wave of change. It was remarkable, how far back the old dears could remember, but they had of course had the full geriatric treatment and they only worked a twenty-five hour week. That left Miryam with plenty to do. Often she'd fetch Lu and Little Em into the lab; she had organized a safe place for him to play and her to sleep if possible, or paddle around, and, as a matter of fact, quite a lot of the students and junior workers quite enjoyed playing with them, so it wasn't too bad. But after work they had to be in her living space, though often the Professorial Mums would get together and have all the children in one space. Sometimes, too, Carlo would take them in his. Or they might all four go to one of the quieter recreation spaces, those which were used mostly by the Professorials; there was one which was well known for being friendly to heterosexual deviants. They felt safe and ordinary there. But it wasn't one of the nicest. They found themselves having long discussions about whether, when the Clones took over the Council, they would be kinder. Or less kind.

'I've got a treat,' said Carlo, fishing in his bag, 'fresh strawberries.'

'Not real ones? From outside? And at this time of year! Oh Carlo! Let's keep one for Lu and another for Little Em. I'll put them behind the curtain for now. It's like the old luxury days when some people got everything, I feel quite wicked! Where did they really come from?'

'They're from the lab gardens, wicked girl! We're working on them. Before you gobble them up, Miryam, have a look at the calyx.'

She twiddled the strawberry round; the deep red was perfect, hard to bruise, yet dissolving on the tongue into juice and scent, but he was right about the calyx. 'That yellow spot? But it isn't on the fruit.'

'Not yet,' said Carlo, 'or rather, not on these.'

'I see. You're working on it?'

'Your people found it first and transferred it to us. We haven't found anything to stop it. At a later stage it gives the fruit a very peculiar taste; they would probably become inedible.'

'Virus?'

'Yes. And not ordinary. In fact, cytologically speaking, of great interest. But it looks a little as though your people have bred out the gene that kept it in its place. Awkward.'

'Very. But what a flavour. With most strawberries you taste it at first and then it goes. This stays.'

'That's the scent-boost. But it may be responsible. The really worrying thing is that this is re-infecting its parents, rather fast; and one of these is Big Love.'

'That's the strawberry they grow everywhere. If it were to go—could it happen this season?' He nodded. 'Then we might have to start again, which wouldn't necessarily be too easy. We've lost far too many varieties. I've been so busy on the cereals that I haven't thought much about the fruits. I don't suppose it will be my section. I expect you're reporting?'

'Yes,' he said, 'we'll have to make a run-down on it. Not all the Council understand but they like to have the data. And they are nice about it, I'll say that. I think we'll need to have a look at some of the rubus hybrids. A pity if some of them went. You've got the sweetest little strawberry stain on your neck, my love. Let me lick it off!'

They were safe and cozy for a while and only occasionally thought of strawberries or of other people. But Miryam wished again that she had a wider bed. It expanded automatically into maximum comfort for one, but was sized for her living space. 'I wonder if it's any use asking for a move,' she said. 'I know they value my work, at least Jussie does, and probably some of the others. It would be reasonable to say one needs more room for thinking. Some people get nearly twice mine, and if the population is dropping as nicely as they say, there must be spaces becoming available.'

'Or if I got a move,' said Carlo, 'then I could take Lu. I'd love that. But I'm afraid they won't do it for me either, though mine's smaller than yours. We get in one another's way rather badly. Black marks.'

'I find it so difficult to go on with work sometimes when I'm back with them. I can't concentrate. Even when they're asleep I'm half listening.'

'Like now.' He pulled the curtain back an inch and looked in gently; she watched him, soft with love. He turned back to her: 'and you don't get enough sleep, my darling. I can see. No thirty hour week for you.'

'I don't mind,' she said, 'if only—if only—'

Somehow the next morning she felt braver. She would

43

speak to Jussie; after all, Jussie had asked her about the
wheats. She had to adjust the video so that it avoided the
curtain. For the moment Lu and Little Em were behind it;
she had made them a kind of construction of lab material
which they were busily pulling apart; Lu had just got the
hang of the screws. Were they going to rush out? Well, if
so—Jussie couldn't eat her. Or could she? Here goes. She
screened up Jussie and got admission at once.

'Jussie,' she said, 'there were one or two things I didn't
tell you about the wheats.'

'Really?' said Jussie, 'I was very happy about the Andean
maize. But I thought you said there were pockets of the old
wheats in Central Asia?'

'Well, there are. All the Vavilov strains, for one thing.
But we are not entirely happy about them—cytologically
speaking. My—my colleague—' She hesitated; Jussie understood how nearly she had said 'my husband', but her face
on the video did not show any shock. '—well, there have
been mutations. If we are ever to have to do reconstructions
of wheat, it will be awkward. Some of the chromosomes
have slipped.'

'I see,' said Jussie, 'but have you any reason to think
reconstruction may be necessary?'

'There could be an epidemic,' said Miryam, 'possibly a
virus. Such things become pandemic in no time, although
we are now hoping to do some more effective isolation. But
you remember what happened to Delight?'

'The mango-peach? Yes, how good it was. And all went
in a season.'

'My colleague is anxious about the rubus family. He will
be reporting to the Council. But I am anxious about the
wheats.'

'Yes, yes. You didn't tell me yesterday?'

Miryam took a deep breath. 'I was worried. It went out
of my memory for the moment. You see, I work under
difficulties.

'Can we help? Or are these—relational difficulties?'

'In a sense.'

'You are considering perhaps the idea of—normalizing?
If we could care in any way? I'd send someone over.
Hormones?'

'No, Jussie, no! But—' Suddenly she shifted the video
round. Lu and Little Em had spilled out of their corner and
the curtain now showed an end of the cot. They were tug-
ging at the construction or what was left of it, Lu in silence
but giggling. Little Em, not yet educated into sharing, with
a yell of rage. 'It isn't always easy to work,' said Miryam
flatly through the yell. 'You value me, don't you? Can't
you give me more living space? Not much, but a little.
Jussie, if you really choose to care, try to do this for me.'
She watched Jussie's face. It gave away nothing. She
reached up for a toy and sent it trundling over the floor.
Lu seized on it with a big laugh, but did at least let Little
Em share.

Jussie tried to look through the video without tenderness
at the children. Why should she be tender? They were not
Clones. They were—worthless. Although there might be
useful Professorial genes in them. No, not to think that;
they were only surplus population. Lu looked back into the
screen and there was a lady staring at him who didn't want
to like him. The laugh went out of his face; his eyes dark-
ened with tears; his lower lip began to tremble. Miryam
turned the video back to herself. 'Well,' she said, 'well,
Jussie?'

'I could find—a nursery—for both of them. They could
be taken away, taken care of, and not bother you. They

would be adequately loved; I guarantee that, Miryam. I realize how difficult—'

'No,' said Miryam, looking straight at her. 'No.'

'I was afraid you'd say that,' said Jussie, 'but think it over, Miryam.'

'Some people have more living space than this. That's true, isn't it?'

Reluctantly Jussie said, 'Yes, that's true.' It was partly accidental. Not all buildings were alike or even dated from the same epoch. Good ones were kept on, especially in Scandinavia. There were some that had balconies looking out over recreation spaces or, more rarely, over food growing spaces. You could see real trees; people who chose to breathe it could have genuine outside air. Even the bath rooms were big and there would be a specially set back and roomy kitchenette, as it was still so romantically called, for the instant ray and the disposer. But none of the Council had this kind of living space; it would have shamed them.

Miryam went on: 'And you want me to go on working at the cereals?'

'Certainly. Perhaps there should be a further search.'

'Well, then.'

'You don't make it easy,' said Jussie. 'If you were living a normal life—even with the children—'

'That isn't how I am, or will be. And I can't be what I'm not.'

'I understand,' said Jussie shortly, and repeated, 'But you don't make it easy.'

'I don't intend to make it easy, Jussie,' said Miryam, and stooped to roll another toy at the children.

'Declaration of war?' said Jussie, but in a friendly way.

'Nonsense,' said Miryam, 'I'm only asking for what I need. Not a luxury. I shan't stop my work for you; I like

46

it. But I want proper thinking conditions. I don't stop weighing up our lab problems when I come back to my living space, any more than you Councillors do with your problems. No, don't let's quarrel, Jussie. Think it over. Will you?'

Think it over. Was it possible to think of anything but Elissa? Who had stepped off into nothing, not to be seen, touched, heard, smelled. Who might or might not come back. Pull yourself together, you are a Councillor. Be good, be understanding, care, remember the Code. Perhaps Miryam was entitled to rather better treatment. Yes, her work was excellent. She was completely loyal except in this one matter, a major one no doubt, but at least she was entirely open about it. Yes, well. 'I'll think it over,' said Jussie. 'Truly, Miryam; and don't worry that you spoke to me. No black marks! And I hope the wheat situation turns out less dangerous than you fear.'

CHAPTER FIVE

R IC had made a music poem and shut it in its capsule. From time to time he looked at it. Yes, it was finished. He was pleased with it. Perhaps he would listen once more before—before it would possibly, in certain contingencies, be allowed to take its message. If the technique of music poems had been available at that time, would Shakespeare have used it for his sonnets? Almost certainly. For the clear case of the first hundred and twenty. And then for centuries he had been thought to be partly deviant! But now the 'dark lady' too was identified, the teaser with his long legs in the Elizabethan trunks and hose, his slim sword—but no doubt he would have been terribly dirty. Not that Will Shakespeare would have been put out by that. Six centuries ago; nothing at all in world time. His mind wandered for a moment to other great lovers: Socrates and Plato, Alexander and Hephaestion, Arjuna and Krishna, Jesus and John, Hadrian and Antinous—*hospes comesque corporis*—Stalin and Beria, though this last was still somewhat uncertain, too many guesses had been made. Away from the Indo-Europeans to the Seven Samurai, to the God-heroes of Oceania, only so recently clarified by the Melanesian research group, or again, the hidden meanings in the tales of the Malian griots handed down since the days of Sundiata.

He thought of great loves wrecked by the social customs of the times : Marx and Engels, poor Charlie and Fred who might have been both happier and deeper thinkers, but who had been unable, in that ambience, to be anything but unhappily married. He thought of Sappho with her Atthis dragged away into marriage, long ago in Lesbos, of Cleopatra and Charmion, her lady who died with her, but political necessity had forced the great Queen into what must have been the torture of hetero-sexual relations with Caesar and Antony. Ric was happy that now, since his talk with Mutumba, he had felt no more of that stupid distaste towards women, but rather an increasing sympathy, seeing them as the worst victims of ancient history. Well, history must be re-made in order to flower profitably and beautifully. Just as flowers and fruit are constantly re-made. He was thinking of his current work on Castro and Che, the scraps of evidence floating and pinned. He smiled a little : could he consider himself as geneticist of history? It would be re-made again in another century, always yielding something new by a re-arrangement of the evidence.

Ric's living space was markedly untidy, but he did much of his work here rather than in the libraries or memory banks. Most of it was desk with micro-film and mini-capsule scanners and runners. But his *toko-no-ma* niche had a very beautiful picture hanging in it, by one of the Japanese masters; odd how all that had gone on. Of course there was also the video; thinking of past unhappiness, he screened up Stig, who still seemed unlike himself. Should he not have a word with the Convenor?

'No,' said Stig. 'Not yet. This isn't a personal worry, Ric. At least I don't think so.'

'Sure?' Ric wondered if he should mention Hiji. How had that gone? No, better not.

'I find myself getting angry, impatient.' Stig frowned into the video.

'More and more unworthy,' said Ric gently, stating a fact.

'Exactly. And anxious. Most of all anxious about the position of the Council. Actually, I was thinking of screening you up, as a historian. When one is working within history, as we are, we sometimes forget how it happened. The pace, above all. We still have so many remains from quite early times, which we have flowed over.'

'Even in ourselves. Do they worry you, Stig?'

'No, they excite me into thinking. Look, Ric, here was the world in the late twentieth century, not so very long ago. There were quite a few major problems. Right?'

'Over-population getting worse. Poor countries getting poorer. Race war and national war. If war, the possibility of total destruction. Where people massed together, alienation. The advertising-amusement industry. The crisis of identity growing with the generation gap : who are we and why?'

'Yes, yes. And remember that in His young days He was right in the middle of the race war and carried the scars always. And She was a doctor.'

'A Mission doctor in India, till the Mission threw Her out and her adult life began. What are you after, Stig?'

'The song says : *they went with the wave.* I'm beginning to wonder what that means. If it has perhaps stopped having any meaning. If it is still there. Or whether we would know a new wave if it came.'

So this was what was making Stig difficult. Ric made some quick judgments. It must be taken very seriously indeed. By himself first : two adults caring for one another. As was laid down. Also if Stig thought this, probably others in the Council would do so soon, getting caught in a mass mood. Which after all only means that Person A with the ability to do B can only do it in historical period X. 'Come over to the Council Library, Stig. We might need pictures. North entrance : right. Give me half an hour, no, an hour, to collect data.'

'Sure you aren't working, Ric?' Stig had looked up and for a moment the shadow was off him. He nearly smiled.

'That's all right. It's something we've got to work out. See you, then.'

Ric switched the video off, picked up a notebook, then, on an impulse slipped the music poem out of its capsule and into the runner. He had to hear it once again. Yes, yes, in the Second movement. Not enough lift—the flutes, was it? He'd got the swirl in the mind, yes; but the possible outcome not clear. If it was to be understood. But should there not be a certain degree of uncertainty, of ambivalence? If Bobbi did not choose to understand it in the sense in which it was written? No, he would have to polish it, and now, if he was to assemble the data for this other, perhaps more important task and show what was meant by going with the wave, he had better hurry. Thinking of the Clone boy, body and mind, he put the music poem back, touched his door shut and went off to the library. Now all his concentration must be on caring for Stig.

Time passed. There had been emphasis on certain historical turning points. Murmured comment. Stig reached over and switched off the picture. The table was littered with memory bank capsules and such changing maps and figures as had to be continuously consulted. 'I knew all this once,' said Stig. 'Some, one forgets. I don't question the rightness of our doing other work besides being on the

Council, but the human mind is at times inadequate. Possibly, too, my work on figures is somewhat deadening. Even a year or two back this recent history made sense. What I seem to have lost is the kind of sense it made.'

'If many people have lost the sense, good people, I mean, although still unworthy as we ourselves are, then we shall have to go with another wave. First having found it.'

'Good people? Good?' said Stig, growling the word to himself, 'that's a difficult concept. In human history it has meant on the whole, other-regarding, and that of course knocks out pride in all its forms, seeking for power and privilege—our main temptation because it disguises itself as working for others—fear, I suppose, in all its forms. But anger, hate?'

'Anger and hate against individuals: they go. Simple aggressions can always be deflected. But we can and must hate wrong institutions.'

'Yet one must learn to understand even alien institutions and to love the individuals who compose them.' Stig muttered to himself. 'As far as one can see now, She did a very remarkable job of understanding these various religions and, so to speak, drawing their fangs. Understanding this strange insistence on an external and constant purpose and existence: made necessary by the dreadful circumstances of the lives people had to live, no doubt. And remaking them into part of the wave, ultimately into Solution Three. But how often She must have been angry!'

'It isn't there,' said Ric, sweeping his hand over the data, 'no anger from Her, only work. Only getting closer.'

'That's the kind of reason why I don't trust history, or rather historians!' said Stig. 'She *must* have been angry.' Ric took it well, even the bite in it; this was part of caring. 'However,' he went on, 'it does appear as if this deep understanding were something Her Clones have inherited, Although it may be less necessary now. What do you think?'

Ric hesitated. 'No. It is necessary still. From time to time there is an attempt to set up a new counter-institution, based on the disorder of irrationals and usually giving power to some group. Stig, did you notice that we had sent off one of Her Clones, a senior one, to monitor and if necessary help Elissa? Of course Elissa herself was not told, nor, by the way, was Jussie, so don't mention it. This isn't simply an experiment. We have lost three; I happen to know because that is my section of the minutes.'

'You count them as expendable?' Stig sounded upset. *'Them?'*

'No, No! Though perhaps they do themselves. As She did. And as you know, in the end— But we haven't begun to know the possibilities. They mayn't be at all what we think. They may be another wave we haven't seen. And by "we" of course I mean us and the computers. One feeds in somewhat surprising material and sometimes the result is not what is expected. Put a few of these surprises together and then perhaps— But in a way your worry is one of the surprises, at least to me. I always felt you were secure, as I think I am. Though one is not one's own best observer.'

Stig said slowly: 'Participation. That's what the other Clones should do. His. And of course Hiji's report bears this out. Answering everyone's Who and Why, making them know who they are, but rationally, not through external unrealities, in the ways the old rites did. Yet again one asks oneself about the temptation to be alone; is it known whether the Clones feel this?' Ric shook his head; but possibly he might yet arrive at this knowledge. 'That isn't exactly fear. To be alone may even be necessary for a time. For thought.'

'It doesn't appear to have been necessary for them as yet,' said Ric, 'not for any I have spoken with.' But was Bobbi perhaps too young to have this need? Yet if it suddenly came on him? Switch off from that. He added : 'I don't suppose we shall know until the Clones take over the Council.'

'Ah !' said Stig suddenly. 'I think I have caught one of my worries. Naturally their taking over is something we've all looked forward to. The Council at last of pure goodness. Without our worries, our unworthiness. Our bad memories and guilt. But mightn't it sometimes be important to have in the Council this very varied unworthiness, and in the process of caring for one another—the way you're caring for me now, which of course is laid down but nevertheless is deep and real—something new comes to light? You remember the old dialectic : thesis, counter-thesis, synthesis and all that? Long words and all superseded, but it is part of our historical inheritance. Or am I incorrect?'

'No. You have every right to speak. But don't you look forward, as I always do, to their actual taking over? Saying goodbye. Walking right out. And we could rest without doubts and anxieties and constant glancing back to the computers and the memory banks? I've thought of it some-times as perfect peace and freedom, in the certainty that they would get everything right.'

'One could die then : rested. But I ask myself if they would never have doubts themselves. After all, they are His and Her genetic continuations, with all the latent capa-bilities and sensitivities. But without experience.'

'Surely. Only doesn't our much greater experience con-stantly hold us back? Haven't we sometimes not taken risks we should have taken? Allowed ourselves to fear? You remember what happened after our Peruvian decision?

We all do. We were desperately anxious and anxiety is almost always fear, even other-regarding anxiety.'

'And again, can we be sure that none of them have been twisted in any way? Even love can twist. Think back to how things went wrong when we attempted to reproduce His and Her stresses and pains in the adolescents!'

Ric bit his lip. Yes, that was what none of them cared to think about. The early As. If it had happened to Bobbi! But he was so much later. 'Yes,' he said, 'perhaps this is something we ought to be considering. You know, the other thing I have looked forward to was that we humans could re-start space exploration, once we had Them in charge.'

Stig nodded. 'No contamination. No fear. No guilt. Yes, I look forward to that too. Not that either of us is likely to be alive!' They both laughed. As if that mattered!

'I suppose the blue-prints are all there,' said Stig, 'waiting until our world is fit to be in touch with others. Away beyond the old space platform, all we dared to keep. But one supposes they need constant revision. That group of the Professorials who are working on them—have we heard lately?'

'I'm not sure. It'll be going into the memory banks.'

'As I recollect we agreed to let them train a Clone group. Shanti would know.'

'She's not back yet. I'll find out. But meanwhile I'm going to feed in your worry to a constructed programme. We'll see if anything comes up that looks like another wave. You don't really know my computer: I've got it very highly sensitized.'

'I think that will be good. Thanks for caring, Ric. The Code.'

'The Code.'

CHAPTER SIX

THERE had been no news of Elissa and things had gone rather badly. A large section of people in her continent had become suddenly and totally unreasonable. Undoubtedly this could be contained by force, quite easily, but that would be the wrong way. Against the code. The Council, however, decided that they would let it be known among all the adult Clones, or at least among those who had received the major part of their education, that there would be a need for practical action. The computers knew exactly where all of them were. It might be difficult to hold back the volunteers, but this could be done. Two days, perhaps less. It would be the first large scale test.

The rest of the Council felt for Jussie. Care was given her, as was laid down. Somehow, Ric felt most able to do this successfully. Since his own care by Mutumba, it had become easy. He had seen the way and now found it quite irrelevant that she happened to be female. In the course of this Jussie had consulted him about a problem of her own, whether she should help one of the deviant but valuable Professorials: in a way which would make her deviation rather easier. But, as it was unlikely that she would ever become normal, this perhaps did not matter. However, there was the question of example. And it was here that

56

Jussie had suddenly said: 'We have to be careful not to become too completely patterned, haven't we?'

It had set up chains of historical recollection in Ric. The areas which had been difficult for the wave were just those which were too patterned and institutionalized. This included the older Communist countries, caste and prejudice-structured India, parts of Africa, and such pockets of South America and even Europe as were still under the domination of the Roman Catholic church—though this body had in fact tried to ride the wave. And failed. It had gone more easily in the broken-patterned capitalist countries where the crisis of identity was cruellest and there was nowhere for people to fit into; it was here that He had struggled and suffered and grown through it and worked change. 'Pattern?' said Ric, 'I'll have to think about that one, Jussie. Yes, flexibility is essential. And it remains that we must care; as was laid down.'

'Including deviants?'

'Even more. Remember what She said in Sydney.' And Jussie had laughed and said she felt helped.

But deep caring always alters people slightly. Jussie, thinking about how she should care for Miryam, thought also about those two children, softening, perhaps, more than was right, and through them imagining the remote future when the world popu-curve could really be seen to drop. So that the mega-cities would be outdated. Oh, what a pleasure to have more space, more gardens, not only for the Clone Mums but for everyone! People could begin to separate out again into small groups and there would be no need for the Council to worry about any recurrence of the identity crisis. And then, well, with a good world, the kind that He and She had thought towards and worked so hard to make, population could be allowed to stabilize. But from what parents? Or should it be always and only the Clones, the proved excellence? Or—or what? No, this was something it was better not to speculate about without the full data.

If they had been looking at the newscasts, the Clone Mums would have known that things had been working out badly in one part of the world. News-truth was part of the code, though it was not put in too much detail. When people can do nothing about a thing there is no point in shouting it at them and volunteers were not wanted except from the highly skilled. When participation was or might be useful, the newscasts were detailed, even though they might be distasteful. But Gisela had not looked at them for days. She was giving Seventy One some of the more complicated toys. Any time now, the Signs would show. She had been back to the library and screened on the instructions so as to be quite sure. Sometimes one of the Mums would rush eagerly to her carer, saying the Signs were there, but it would turn out she'd made a mistake. But Gisela wasn't going to be made to look silly that way! Her own special carer had been full of encouragement and finally said that she had consulted at a higher level and here was a list of suitable names for later on : would Gisela choose? This would be a permanent bond and when Seventy One came back after his strengthening she would be able to see him and tell him that his name, which would now mean so much to him, had been her choice. 'I do wonder what he'll be like!' said Gisela and took the list out with her. Of course she had to consult Lilac! But how was it Lilac hadn't been given a list?

'Not me,' said Lilac, 'I'm not a top Mum!'

'Why ever not?' said Gisela. 'I can't think. You're so much cleverer than me, Lilac.'

58

'Perhaps they don't want us too clever,' said Lilac, sideways.

'No, I can't see! The things you've told me, Lilac—things I'd never-ever have thought of! Only you aren't watching for Signs the way I am.'

'Gisela,' said Lilac, 'did they ever tell you about the strengthening? All that's going to happen to Seventy One?'

'I know it's bound to hurt my poor little darling, don't pretend I haven't thought, but he'll come out in the end. He'll have had what makes him—you know, properly Him.' Gisela looked round, uncomfortably, not wanting to have to say all this or even think it. Couldn't Lilac let it alone like everyone else?

But no, that was just what Lilac wouldn't do. Lilac threading together real flowers from the picking beds. For what might be the last time: no picking of real flowers in the real world! That would be—luxury. Wrong. A kind of aggression. Lilac dangled a chain of blossoms. 'So it's all going to happen to Seventy One. Did you ever say to yourself, Gisela, that when you see him again he may have got the feeling that you betrayed him, taking away your love suddenly, sending him off to the strengthening like—like a stranger?'

'But won't he be grateful? I'm sure all the Clones are glad it happened to them. They all know it has to be done.'

'Know and feel: different, aren't they?'

Gisela wriggled: 'It's not fair, putting it that way. I just know you've got it wrong, Lilac! They said to me I'd been extra good, all the time. My own carer and Jussie, both of them said so. I might have another turn later. That would be so wonderful! But then—if you weren't with me—do you remember when we first met, Lilac?'

'I'll remember your hair always,' said Lilac, 'the sun

59

was in it. The real sun here in the gardens. You soft thing.'
She looked hard and critically at Gisela: 'Sometimes I wish
you were a plain girl, Gisela.'

'Oh, why? Why ever?'

'Perhaps I'd stop wanting to touch you.'

They looked at one another and Gisela's eyes filled with
tears. 'You know where to video me—if I see the Signs
first?'

'It's written down,' said Lilac, 'besides, I'll remember.
And I'll be back in the computer rooms: CXS. I—I hope
you won't forget—for any reason.'

'How could I forget? But there'll be celebrations for us
both first. Would you like to go on a plane ride over the food
fields? I would. And I'd like to do the big Mega-cit-tour.
There's lots I haven't seen. You know, I'd like to spend a
whole day in the Caves, listening to music poems. At least
I would if you were there. I couldn't listen properly in the
old days before—before you, Lilac.' She looked away and
the blush went creeping up her neck. 'I suppose I'm different now. Tell me what you're going to like.'

'I'd like to go over the mountains. You know, Gisela,
there are still mountains where there isn't anything growing. Nothing at all. No food. No people. Miles and miles
of high, sharp mountains. Snow on the top.'

'Oh I'd be scared! I'm not like you. I mean—really to
see nothing. It's all right on the pictures for then you can
look away. And with the sea there are always the food
stations. But why don't they pull the mountains down?'

'They can't do that. Not yet anyway. And it's rock, not
food earth. It would have to be treated, oh ever so much.'

'When the Clones take over they'll be able to. Won't
they?'

'Perhaps they won't want to. Once the popu-curve starts

dropping there won't be so much need for food. The food fields might—grow flowers—for picking. But perhaps they'll try to make food more special. My Mum says that her Mum's Mum remembered swallowing real milk and real meat from dead animals.'

'I wouldn't like that. Milk from cows, all hairy, the way they are in the library! Honestly, I'd be sick. Wouldn't you?'

'I'd like to try it,' said Lilac thoughtfully, 'and even meat. Cutlets, my Mum's Mum said. You'd have to get used to the smell. But I know I could. It would be a change.'

'Unbalanced,' said Gisela, with great decision for her. What she meant was something stronger. Lilac was trying to shock her! Trying? Yes, she had! It had been a long time since people had stopped eating their fellow animals. This was mostly, no doubt, that they were such inefficient makers of protein and fat or milk constituents, but partly civilized sentiment. In normal circumstances, causing the death of any vertebrate was highly distasteful, especially if it was for food. There were still the various wild spaces, mountain, forest, desert, swamp or hard permafrost, in which the flora and fauna were carefully preserved and people only allowed as a privilege or reward. Here, just occasionally, some animal had to be killed and even eaten. People who had actually had this experience felt themselves for a time cut off, almost deviant. It was not something one talked about. Yet a few found it interesting, enabling them to think differently, or, more often, to arrive at some new aesthetic concept.

Lilac had once met a woman who'd had this type of experience in a wild space and who had afterwards written a poem which had been both admired and hated. Some had even wanted the Council to take action, but they had said it was entirely out of their competence. Lilac had thought of this poem on and off and wished she'd had the nerve to get together with the woman who'd written it, so that she could ask her lots of questions and share how she'd felt. She had not let it interfere with her computer programming, but during her almost three years in the gardens and seeing real animals, even if they were gentle and half humanized, she had remembered it and even dreamed about it. Dreamed about killing. Straight aggression, not deflected. What did that mean? She hadn't had these dreams before she'd been a Clone Mum. Were they—resentment? She couldn't talk about them, above all not to Gisela. They were so horrible and yet—she couldn't even make up her mind that she didn't want them.

But now she went back to what she had said earlier and suddenly she wanted more than anything to surprise Gisela, to stick a burning torch into the softness and fairness. 'They'll do some nasty things to our babies, Gisela,' she said, 'cruel. You know, they'll cry for us. Their Mums. And we won't be there.'

Gisela, predictably, began to cry herself. 'Don't!' she said. 'Don't! You know it's not cruelty. It's strengthening. They've got so much to do for the whole world, when they're—Him, or Her of course.'

'Look,' said Lilac, leaning closer. 'Have you ever thought what He would have been like without that conditioning in His young days, all we know He had to go through? He mightn't have had the strength to ride the wave; He mightn't have been able to gather people to be with Him. He mightn't have been able to change things as we know He did. But then, He might have been a marvellous painter or a musician or a scientist—'

'You can't say He could ever have been a Professorial!'

said Gisela, deeply upset. Lilac was going altogether too far.

'Well, perhaps not. Not the way we think of them. If He had been, He would have been different. He'd have dug into finding out, the way they do, but He couldn't have criticized the Code the way they do—well, of course, if He had been one, then there wouldn't be a code because He wouldn't have made it! And I don't mean, Gisela, I know we can't think of Him having—having relations—but listen! Supposing His mind had been set to looking at those sort of problems instead of the problems He did look at— and the same for Her. They were both—well, superior. We know that, it was in the genes.' Lilac was rushing at it, trying to get it clear to herself, and Gisela stared, not quite understanding or willing to understand. 'But supposing They'd not had the strains and stresses which are what we're told the strengthening is intended to be like, supposing They'd only had kindness, well then, what would They have been? Different. Different. You know what it says in the books. At one period He showed what they call artistic leanings, but the way things were He had to go out and work.'

'To make a better world for us all!'

'But now it's made. And why should they have to go through it all again? Why? They're superior, yes, we know that, but they could be superior in something else. Look, Gisela: I want my Ninety to be a composer, a marvellous composer who'll make us all laugh and cry and shiver. Or the best painter there's ever been! Doing something so new we can't even begin to imagine it!' She was panting now.

'But they've got to be Him—just the same!'

'No. There's something I've thought of. Look, we don't speak His name because—because power shouldn't have a name. Any sort of power. Even the best power. But painters are named, writers, musicians, they're against power so they all have names which can be loved. Don't you want that for Seventy One, not just a name out of the list? That's what I want for my sweetie!'

'But you can't, you just can't!' said Gisela. 'There'll be the Signs coming—any day now!'

Lilac whispered straight at her: 'And suppose I don't tell?'

Gisela went very white and then gradually blushed as though she'd been too hard kissed. 'If you don't tell I shall have to,' she said, and then, 'Oh Lilac, my darling, come back, come back to me! You've gone away, you've had these terrible thoughts, but listen. If you won't be sensible, I'll try to be sensible for you! One of the watchers would see the Signs even if you managed to hide them somehow or another; it would only be a matter of time, a few days, a week. And then, if you haven't told them yourself, they'll be so angry. They—they might do anything! Because you'd be doing wrong, dreadfully wrong, worse than the Professorials—no, I must say it! Don't ever think again of doing this. Can't you see, Lilac, if you did I would have to speak to someone!'

'But you can't, Gisela,' said Lilac gently, and looked at her deep down below the blush. 'You can't. Because you love me.'

'I'd do it because I loved you—'

'No. No. You love me like I love Ninety. I can't hurt him. You can't hurt me. A girl doesn't just betray someone she loves. She helps them instead. She wouldn't tell anyone. Would she? Would she?'

'No,' whispered Gisela, twisting a bit. 'No, I suppose not.'

CHAPTER SEVEN

CARLO looked again at the plates, all of them, even the semi-discarded. There might be something, some clue. One must look and look. The data fed to the computers were accurate, but supposing there was some small indication which had utterly not been considered? There were some slides he wanted to think about; he adjusted, felt about mentally. No. No. His team had brought in specimens of almost every rubus; so many had been hybridized over the years, especially the roses.

For he was beginning to have a horrid suspicion that cultivated roses might be involved. This would be a blow. They were grown so much in all the temperate area recreation spaces, and they had been bred for miniature pots in living spaces, great attention going to the scent. New ones were always being invented. Which sometimes meant going back to the wild types. What else? Amazing how many of the favourites were in rosaceae : apple, pear, cherry, plum, peach and almond. Raspberry and blackberry of course, with all their hybrids. This virus would have, if possible, to be contained. Well, they'd had that out at the Staff meeting. There was of course no infection pool of old orchards, as there would have been a century ago. But still, it would need administrative action from the top and the Council appeared to be much involved in their latest trouble : what would have been called a rebellion in the old days. They would have to wake up and attend to this, which was probably more important.

One of the team of young Clones came in; as always he moved so quietly that for a moment Carlo didn't see him. Then he came across with his delightful, disarming smile of curiosity and friendship and joined Carlo at the bench. The Clones had the complete right to ask questions. All the labs knew that and collaborated. It was always a pleasure; it seemed to make their work completely worthwhile. Professional, skilled participation? Yes, no doubt. Written in the DNA and all that. But how it worked! And when they take over the Council they will remember our lab. That of course was what any of the labs, to which a Clone group had been assigned, thought, and all knew that the other labs thought it too. So, in terms of power it cancelled out, but in terms of smooth-running, heightened interest and free flow of ideas, it worked.

It seemed odd sometimes that when the Clones were there, painful Professorial jealousies seemed to ease down and become totally irrelevant. Even the feeling that now one could say anything and it would be taken simply for what it was, emptied the suspicion out of working and social contacts, far beyond the lab doors. Carlo almost felt that he could speak about Miryam and the children, but wasn't totally sure. The Clones were so young; there was experience which they had not yet had directly, even though much of it had been programmed into them during sleep. But it was not yet certain how this corresponded with real, that is unexpected, experience, with uncertainty as to the outcome. And how to find out? Impossible directly, but feasible by observing whether a new situation was perceived

66

and handled as though it had already been experienced and overcome.

There was the usual difficulty about assessment. The Clones themselves were of course extremely adept at putting their own reactions into words, but even so there was an element of personal judgment. Well, that would doubtless take time to find out; the subliminal programme was constantly being altered and adjusted. A fascinating job for another lab team.

Meanwhile Carlo demonstrated his material to Kid, the Clone boy, and Kid asked the kind of questions that showed he had understood, that he was even racing ahead, and also that he had mentally assessed and remembered the technical terms. He had been joined by another of the Clone group, Maggie, her long hair in plaits, her face pale and serious. Both of them, like the rest of the Staff, wore plain lab spray-ons of a heavy protective. She too had the clonal outstanding memory for a once heard or apprehended fact. There was plenty of work still to be done on memory and the Professorial quarrels of two centuries earlier were by no means over, though they had changed in the sense that there was far more material to quarrel about. Carlo thought of this briefly and grinned to himself, being glad to be on what was at present relatively uncontroversial cytology. But how calm they were, Maggie and Kid, these bits of the future. And if their abilities could be joined? One of her plaits fell for a moment over his hand; he flicked it away. And Carlo, having let the thought come fleetingly into his mind, suppressed it with a stroke of will: impossible to allow even a deviant thought in front of them! Though probably they were quite immune to it.

Had they ever, he asked them, seen pictures of some of the rarer rubus hybrids? He doubted it, but they only had

67

to hear the names once for them to stick. The classification of the rosaceae was a matter of moments, and also their appreciation of what was endangered. For one or two of the hybrids he had quite a number of spare fruits, not yet attacked by the virus. They tasted them with interest and a fresh pleasure—how delightful to please them! Not that it mattered in the least compared with the demonstration and questioning, but yet they were, somehow, all the world's children. All the intelligent and responsible world.

Carlo heard a tiny buzz from his wrist audio; he lifted it and listened: Miryam, her voice rather high and agitated. They scarcely ever communicated during working hours. 'I'm wanted for a field trip,' she said. 'Yes, wheats. Central Asia. Have to leave tonight. Think I can get Lu fixed up. Can you take Little Em? Over.'

'Of course. Don't worry. I'll be with you in an hour. How long will you be away? Over.'

'Uncertain. I'm getting my injections now. We'll talk. Finish.'

He looked up, troubled, to read sympathy from the two Clones. How near he was to telling them! 'It's a colleague with whom I'm working,' he said, 'going off on a field trip. Central Asia, she says. I have to take over some of the materials.'

'We understand,' said Maggie. 'Work comes first. We'll cover the plates and put the slides in order. Yes, we know how! But perhaps Kid and I could have another look? We won't eat the fruit!'

One of Miryam's deviant friends was there. She had deflated the cot and bed and was packing. Lu, whom she was taking with her, was in tremendous spirits, jumping and questioning, but Little Em was a bit tearful. How was he going to fit her into his living space, which was slightly smaller than Miryam's? Actually, she herself would be no problem, but a child has to take around some of its world for security and peace of mind. And small children tend to get attached to large objects! He must take some to avoid the danger of Little Em getting imprinted with his own image. 'You haven't heard from Jussie?' he asked quickly, helping her to pack; the injections were still sore, but should give her a 100% immunity for the regions where she was going. No spray-ons for field work; she was already wearing her overalls in tough synthetics, with temperature adjustment.

Miryam shook her head. 'No. She screened me once, but it was about something else. I'm afraid it's no use. You'll remember that Little Em can't manage the sulphur proteins? Goodness knows why. They ought to be all right but they just aren't. If you're stuck—'

'But I shan't be, love.' And if I am, he thought, I'll just tell the Clones. It will be a nice new problem for them. But of course I couldn't. Anyhow, I shall manage—one baby! Nothing. I shall enjoy having her.

So there was Miryam off to Ulan Bator on the first hop of the flight, Ulan Bator no longer a city of black felt yurts and horses and camels, but block after high block of Moscow-type living spaces, though a few on the outer edge still had windows that looked out over the immense plain, now mostly in wheat, but with some leguminous crops, and the tall well and irrigation structures here and there towards the horizons. Wheat, rather ominously standard, all the same height, colour, genetic formula, tailored to its environment.

The next morning she screened Carlo up expensively on the two-way, but probably that was covered by the expedition: colleagues must be able to consult. 'The moment we arrived they insisted we come to the live theatre, very interesting, all heroic ancient history, stereo yurts, swords, spears, and real horses, yes, they insist on that, all the old songs, Cheng was interpreting and they were really most extraordinary—talk about aggression! The audience went simply mad. There were two Clone girls there, experiencing, and of course they roared and stamped too. So we all did, there was no harm or danger in it; the aggression was completely deflected. Only I was still rather tired and kept thinking of you. Have you found any more virus hosts? Anything you want specially looked for? Yes, I'll keep my eye open; a lot of things start in central Asia. How's my Little Em?'

'Fine. But I can't get her to look at you. She's listening and looking all round, but I can't get her to focus on the screen.'

'Oh my little silly! Quite sure you're all right with her? I mayn't be able to get in touch for a bit—'

So that was that. Everything would be all right. She had been on expeditions before. Cheng was a first-rate interpreter. But, as the days went by, Little Em began to be not quite so fine. She wouldn't eat, though he tried all sorts of things, keeping well off sulphur proteins. Carlo was worried. She'd had all the basic inoculations. What was making her cry? The old ladies at the lab nursery were fussed. Instead of coming eagerly to Carlo as she always used to do, she kept lying on her face, pulling her knees up and yelling or whimpering. They felt her for lumps or hardness or scratches. Nothing. And he just had to go back and check some of his material. Living things have a habit of changing behind your back. The clock must be observed.

When he looked up, Kid was there again. 'What is it?' he said. 'Please let me care.'

70

'Why do you suppose there's anything wrong?' said Carlo, controlling his voice and hands.

'I do know,' Kid said. 'You needn't hide. You've taught me, so your trouble is mine. Please tell.'

Carlo looked away. 'One has one's worries,' he said, 'when one's older.' Kid came close and suddenly Carlo found himself thinking, well, why not? And then, do him good! Wanting to disturb the red-brown smile, the clear onyx of the innocent eyes. Here goes. 'I'm anxious about my little girl,' he said levelly. 'She doesn't seem well and I'm not sure what it can be.' He watched Kid adjust, shift into another gear. Poor Kid! No, one couldn't be sorry for a Clone. They had the future.

'Should she go to a health clinic?' said Kid.

'I don't think so. She had all the inoculations. There's no fever or any symptoms I can find. But she can't explain; she's only just over a year old.'

'Then—her mother—' Kid was fumbling, but his smile stayed, unshocked, reassuring.

'Off on a field expedition, a sudden call. I told you I had a colleague going to central Asia. My wife is a plant geneticist.' There, let Kid have the whole thing, straight in his face!

Kid seemed to give a little swallow, then he had accepted the new fact. 'Do you think your little girl is—lonely? What's her name?'

'We call her Little Em.' Curious, he was now feeling that this was quite a normal situation and conversation.

'Could I see her? It just could be that one of us could get through to her. Can't be sure, but—now you're saying to yourself, that cat might hurt my baby.' Yes, so he had! 'But I won't try anything I shouldn't. Maybe you'd give me a few details just for fill-in? It would kind of help.

Now you're thinking maybe I've said plenty and too much. But look, you've been teaching me : seems to me I know a bit more cytology now. You didn't hold back. That's how I'd like to care for you, and the ones you love, whoever they are. It's new to me.' The Clone boy looked at him engagingly, asking, almost, for a favour.

'All right,' said Carlo. 'I'll tell you. And I'd like you to see Little Em; she's in the lab nursery just now; the old dears there are worried too. Come along, Kid.' He began to tell about Miryam, trying to be completely calm and unemotional, staring in front of him as they walked down the wide, light passage with the centrifuges and heating or refrigeration units, all the things he knew so well. Colleagues nodded or called across to him. One of them came out of a side room and said, 'Look'. It was a cherry, the yellow spot, starting at the stalk, was beginning to mottle the dark, shining fruit.

'You're going through the routine tests?' Carlo asked. 'Fine. I'll be back. What's the betting now? Plum?'

'Seems it'll be a synthetics summer,' said the colleague.

The Clone boy walked on beside Carlo, apparently not disturbed by what could well be his first deviant situation. They left the lab and took the express walk-way over to the genetics building, and past the show beds of the newest tulips which now went on for four months in the year. Still Carlo spoke of Miryam, not looking round, and still the Clone boy walked beside him with a look of great interest. Then through a door, past two little pot roses, pink and white—but how long would it be before the virus showed on them?—and into the nursery and the sound of miserable, exhausted sobbing. Kid settled down on the floor beside Little Em and began to talk to her. For a minute she flounced away, on to her other side, crying louder; he put his hand where hers could grab it, first in anger, then in interest. The crying began to ease off. She almost opened her eyes to look. Participation? 'O.K.,' said Kid, flashing up a smile at Carlo, 'think I can care right!'

CHAPTER EIGHT

'BUT Ric,' said Bobbi, 'of course I love you. Why are you so anxious?'

'You—you heard my poem?'

'Yes, it was beautiful music, so beautiful. I just don't know how you do it. The sounds; I don't even know how some of them are made. And then the words. You showed your love for people. That does good to hear.'

'I wouldn't say it was people, Bobbi. Didn't you understand?—it was you.'

'But I'm people. You call us the Clones but that doesn't signify; we don't want to be different. Truly I don't much like it, to be called a Clone with the kind of voice not-Clones use. We're all part of one another. You're one of the Council, Ric. You know that. It's your work, participating.' He looked puzzled, vulnerable, like most of the young Clones. He wore, not a spray-on, but the archaic dress which He could have worn, open-necked T shirt and pants of non-synthetic genuine cotton. Apart from the lab teams assigned to learn from the Professorials, most of the Clones dressed this sort of way. The smooth brown of his neck rose in a lovely column from the blue shirt; a little muscle jumped at the side. If I could touch it, thought Ric, only touch, only once. 'What I thought about your music poem,

74

Ric,' said Bobbi, 'and mind, I'm no expert on music, haven't had that education yet, was that it was in some way tense. It's a love poem : right. But love's a giving thing, surely? It flows easy, between us all.'

'It hasn't done that always,' said Ric.

'Ah now, that's history and I get to wonder sometimes if it's been seen like it sure was or like we think it should have been. These cats—' Ric had changed the art object in the *toko-no-ma*. Today it was a piece of sculpture : some young hero, Pythias, Alkibiades, Hephaestion, did it matter which?—'did they count it the way we're taught they did? Didn't history just go on past them?'

Ric was finding it hard to concentrate. He wanted to say to Bobbi that he was more beautiful, moving around, than the still stone of the statue. But how could he say it without frightening the bird of heaven that had stooped towards him? Slowly he answered : 'Certain kinds of people and their relationships are the flowerings of historical periods. One could not exist without the other.'

Earlier the boy had told him how much he had wanted to go with the others to the point of world disturbance for which they had asked for volunteers, but they had said he was not old enough; he had not finished his education. It was in the process of caring and cheering him up about this (though Bobbi had accepted it perfectly reasonably) that Ric had produced the music poem capsule, and, while it was playing, felt a profound thankfulness—but thankfulness to what, to whom, the Council members who had turned him down or something, someone, quite else?—that Bobbi had not been taken. 'Why don't you stay here for a day or two and look at my history books?' he asked, as lightly as he could.

But Bobbi said, 'No, I've a pad fixed with the rest and

we do a bit of talk over history learning. Though I'd like fine to do a go-through of some of these books you have.' He moved among them, slipped one into the scanner and watched for a minute while Ric, pretending to look for another, watched him. Then he turned and asked suddenly : 'Ric, how come you're on the Council?'

'You really want to know?' But of course! One accepted that the Clones were speaking truth. 'Well,' said Ric, 'it was like this, but I have to go back a bit. You know, after the Aggressions, there was a lot destroyed. In all the cities. Some of it was—of great value to the world. Beautiful, irreplaceable. There were things of which we don't even have pictures. We only know they existed. You've seen some of the destruction yourself.' Bobbi nodded; it had been part of his strengthening. Painful. His guides had seen to that. 'Yes, after the clearing up enough was left to show people that aggressions must not happen any more. But there was a lot of material which survived—underneath, for instance.'

'Was it safe to get?' Bobbi asked. Is he concerned about me, thought Ric, or merely interested?

'There were certain precautions that had to be taken, even after a number of years. Tests had to be made. That was routine. Well, I was working on that. We had museums and libraries to clear up and, for instance, these were mostly the old type books, printed and bound and heavy. Half of it was rubbish and could be discarded, but there had to be someone who knew about them. A lot of people weren't interested. The Council were in being by then, as you know, and were reformulating and modifying population policy, although Solution Two had begun to show results. The idea of reasonably equal living spaces had been accepted gradually, but not everywhere. There were always pockets of genuine misunderstanding and also groups here and there who tried to assume privilege and had to be dealt with.'

'By violence? I seem to remember—'

'As far as possible not. But the Council sometimes had to use it. As they may have to use it yet; it is not entirely ruled out—anywhere. Violence without hate: it is possible. Bear it in mind, Bobbi, that, although some of the Council had the supreme advantage of having actually seen and known Him and Her, they did not have the bigger advantage of all of you growing up. There had been some bad failures of biological method, not so much by the physiologists (though there were failures there too) as by the psychologists who could not get the pressures right.'

'The pressures?'

'The strengthening. Bobbi, I never liked to ask you, but—'

'It's over.' Bobbi shook his head, frowning a little. 'Don't ask, please.'

'No. Well, at that time there were only a very few young Clones who seemed . . . in a satisfactory state . . . on coming back into the world. Most of you were yet to be created. Meanwhile the Council were roping in anyone with special knowledge and who seemed, well, non-deviant. And of of course administratively committed: not a Professorial. Though there has always been some fluidity of movement. I had become deeply interested in aggression: the roots, the trigger-off, the effects of over-small groups too closely and competitively dependent on one another and over-large groups not sufficiently dependent. In fact I worked for some time with the Amerindians who had not yet been drawn into the population policy, but who provided a marvellous field experiment with groups. It seemed to the Council that aggression control was a vital part of the population long-term policy which was then being re-organized.'

77

'But it had been working for a long time, Ric! After all, it was before the aggressions and at the big height of the old population crisis that males and females were taught to draw apart. Solution One: O.K. People got to know it was the fully human way of living. And once this was seen clear it hit everybody, just everybody. It's in the books, in the films. It was the end of all that pain!'

'Yes, yes, you know your history, Bobbi. But things are never that simple.' And yet, he thought, for the Clones, so innocent in the basic sense of the word, things might be simple. He reached over and swung Bobbi's cool brown hand: so little in it but yet, to him, so much. 'No policy is right forever. Only the Code, which isn't policy, but a way to think about things. There has to be constant flexibility—' He thought now of his talk with Stig, which of them had said that? '—We tend to get into patterns. And there is the danger of one pattern 'rousing hate—aggression— against another.' Now he remembered what Mutumba had said about that, when she was caring for him. 'You see, about the code. We take it for granted but it wasn't always there. Actually, She had left notes for it, which we try to follow. But there were questions of interpretation; She referred to books which nobody had heard of; some had been destroyed. She had even occasionally used a kind of medical shorthand. It was thought that I was good at this interpretation.'

He stopped speaking. He was remembering now a much further back meeting with Mutumba; her hair was black then, though, oddly, a different black to that of the Clone boys. She had volunteered as a Clone Mum in the days when things did not always work out too well either for the Clone or for the Mum and she was heavily pregnant, with deep lines round her eyes. But she was really a better interpreter of the code than he was, with a strange way of guessing just what She meant. That was why she had asked for her Clone to be Her's.

It was Mutumba incidentally, who had organized the disposal of the precious living tissues to a number of centres where there would be slightly different methods of culturing them. The gardens for the Mums had not been laid out or even thought of then, and Mutumba had given birth, with some complications, he knew, in one of the original clinics. And the Clone had been perfectly all right, the little flax-haired scrap they had all gone to see, since Mutumba was already in the Council, though one of the younger members. A Sixteen. It was only the ones who were physiologically perfect who were given numbers. And life. The Clone girl must be fully adult by now, her education and experience finished. Unless of course the psychologists had gone wrong later over her strengthening. This happened less often with the females since Her stresses during life had been different from His and apparently easier to picture out on the pre-adult girl. Well, one would probably never know what happened to her or where she was now. Nor would Mutumba. In those days there was no contact between Mum and Clone after the separation. The new policy was different, but they were not yet certain if it was wise.

Bobbi was looking at him curiously. What kind of curiosity? Non-aggressive certainly. But at what point does non-aggression change to love? He wanted to go on telling Bobbi how, because of his interest in the old books and other historical material, he had lately developed his special computer which had style and clarity—the kind of clarity that a great poem has, immediately recognized. But that came later, almost two decades after he had first joined the Council. In the early days there had been the clearing up of concepts: non-aggression not the same as non-violence. One dived into history to hunt for the clues. There had been all these essential built-in mechanisms for stopping intra-specific aggression which mankind has broken again and again, so often with individualized sex as the trouble maker. All must be reinterpreted and these reinterpretations of the old mechanisms are the great steps of history. Inter-sexual love, resulting in the birth of children, had been necessary. When it not only ceased to be necessary, but was seen as a menace, then the logic of history made itself felt. The challenge to aggressive inter-sexual love came first from Her; then the challenge was made still clearer in the Code which He homologated and by the Council itself. When that age-old sexual aggression changed to non-aggressive love of man for man and woman for woman, overt aggression dropped in the same curve as the still dropping popu-curve. But between individuals there was still uncertainty. Not aggression, not violence, but the lovely uncertainty of the heart.

'Explain how you make a music poem,' said Bobbi suddenly.

Ric laughed. He must have written twenty music poems in his life, not including the first attempts. All had begun from some intense awareness of an object, not necessarily a person, though at least three had been about persons whom he had loved. The object of the poem was not necessarily beautiful, but to be made into a certain kind of experience. And this experience must be completely communicable in a different category; that was what a music poem was about. Bobbi listened and while he listened he moved about the room, rippling under the open-necked shirt like wind over the food fields. You might see the ripples better through a spray-on, but with less of a heart choke. 'Play it again, Ric,' he said. And again Ric fitted it into the slots. But the Second movement? Perhaps he should have worked on it more. Perhaps he should have played it to Stig. Yes, perhaps when there was next a free meeting-time he would do just that. He knew that Stig had written at least two music poems which he had never heard. Yes, he would like to hear them.

'Is it the same as painting a still-picture?' asked the Clone boy, again with the curiosity of someone who has not yet had full aesthetic experience.

'It is more durable, you know, Bobbi. After all, most still pictures are painted in the great painting halls all over the world by young people and they get tired of them and off they go. Just once in a long while something is made which seems fit to keep and be looked at by others, which achieves communication in its own medium. You've been in the painting halls, Bobbi, haven't you?'

'Us cats doing fun. Yes. But not for too long. Once we'd made all the colours and seen what the shapes come to, then there wasn't what we wanted. Except maybe one or two. There was this Elsie, she kept picking things to pieces, a real flower, say, or the insides of machinery, and setting it down the way she thought it was. Maybe the way she felt it would be if she was inside herself. I couldn't figure— not yet—why she did that. Only one wanted to go back and look at her pictures again. And sometimes she'd have chucked them in the disposer. Why?'

'It was in the DNA, you know, Bobbi. I would always think this might happen to Her Clones. We know, for instance, that She was good at anatomical drawing; there are one or two notebooks extant. You don't have that in your genes.'

81

'Funny,' said Bobbi, 'there's a lot I don't understand yet. History. Books. Thanks for letting me hear that music poem, Ric. I'm glad you love people.'

At the door he turned, with a warm gentle smile to Ric and then back to his own people, where he belonged, among his equals. Ric was left empty, empty. Oh my unworthiness, oh my Second Movement! How did he not hear?

CHAPTER NINE

A T last the news was coming in, reliably and in quantity. After the first screenings Mutumba had sent out calls for which ever of the Council were available. Certain decisions would have to be made. Negotiations and persuasion could start; it would now be possible to find negotiators on the other side whose minds were not clouded. Through the morning, Council members came quickly from wherever they were working. Most of them had been kept fairly well in touch with what had been happening, but when they met there was a quick screen-through of essentials.

It appeared that the disturbance, the aggressions, had been contained, and with the minimum of force. Skilled understanding had been used by the Clones in whose genes this lay. Participation in the expressions of aggression had led to knowledge of its roots. Then the cure could be attempted, and this was already begun. Harm had been done, as was inevitable. But now there must be dialogue. The victims of aggression were not only those on whom it had been used, but those who had used it. 'There are men and women whom we shall have to meet and talk with, according to the Code, without hate,' said Mutumba, formally, gathering the Council members with her eyes, 'but first we shall have the full report and questions.'

Jussie stood up and said, 'You yourself have had the first report?' Mutumba moved her head in assent. 'You said: without hate. I take it that our Council member is—dead.'

Mutumba looked very gravely straight at Jussie. 'Yes, Elissa is dead. Without her death the aggression could have continued, maximally.'

'Whose report, then?' Jussie asked. She knew, now, that she had thought it might happen; then, that it had happened. There had been happiness. There had been delight. Out of delight, even for so short a time, love had grown. It was good that there had been love. Fleetingly she wondered whether Elissa's own delight and confidence in her powers had made her take risks. But useless and stupid to hurt herself with this.

'One of our Clones, a B, is reporting,' said Mutumba, 'her name is Anni.' The young woman, Anni, came in and greeted the Council; she was wearing blue overalls and a white shirt and she carried one arm a little stiffly, as though it had been hurt. If it had been Elissa she would have worn a wild spray-on. Her small golden ears. Elissa must be coming! No.

The report was long and factual. Occasionally Anni put down her head to her wrist note-recorder to remind herself of the sequence. The Council watched her very carefully; it was the first time one of the Clones had reported on anything of vital importance. Was she completely competent? Yes, they thought so. She went quickly through the early stages, answering occasional questions. One or two Council members were still coming in. There were about twenty present and some others had been contacted and would easily join in the discussion by video. It happened that there had been a conference of interested members, computers and a few Professorials on the possible outcome of shortening the general temperate zones thirty hour week, something which could easily be done, but might have unforeseen results. Foreseeing, however, was a computer's job. This Conference was being held on one of the favourite island sites with a de-polluted beach and a riding shoal of charming dolphins and was something of a soft option, since it would probably end up in a memorandum by the few members and co-opted Professorials who were genuinely interested. All came to the video, one or two still wet and sandy. But many members were away on missions where they had deliberately covered themselves against interruption or identification.

All listened to Anni's run-through; coming from her Clone mind it was somewhat different from the way they had first seen it. One of the new religions had been at the back of it, a synthetic, in ultimate origin an incoming Hindu sect, thought completely defunct and in essence and every way deviant and boiling with aggression. Anni described this; some found it sickening. There had been the usual build-up of apparent miracles, prophecies, denunciations. Old words like imperialism had been dug up and polished. Clearly the educational methods which had been used by the world government experts had been quite inadequate.

She turned to the very immediate past. What had gone wrong was, as they could see, this and this. The remedies might have been that. Things had gone rather too far by the time Elissa arrived. There should have been an earlier recognition of the crisis, but those who had failed were also dead. Subsequent action, both by Elissa and the Clone volunteers who came out, had been correct, but it was probable that too much trust had been given to an appar-

ently non-deviant group. It was in the course of the participation in and deflection of aggression, that Elissa's identity
had been disclosed and the remains of the aggression had
been directed onto her.

'How did she die?' Jussie asked harshly and the Clone
girl hesitated perceptibly, glancing at Mutumba.

'It is over,' Mutumba said, 'It is history. I shall tell you
anything you want to know—later.'

'They did things to her,' said Jussie. 'I know.' But the
others, the Council, were round her, caring, caring. If it had
happened to herself she would want it forgotten. The hideous
things deviants did. Otherwise it would arouse—counter-
aggression. Yes. Yes.

Anni went on soberly with her story. That was the
moment when the mechanisms of deflection went into
action; the prophets were caught and discredited, the
miracles explained. At this point some violence was necessary. Anni explained exactly what and how. The Clone
men had apparently used great skill and brilliant improvis-
ation. One or two of the Council were reminded of
incidents in His early life.

'You will note,' said Mutumba, 'that at this point the
Clones were working on their own. I think without fear?'

'We knew what had to be done,' said Anni, 'it was
obvious. It would have hindered us to feel fear. But there
is much still to be done. The Council wants us to stay?'

Mutumba looked round at her colleagues: 'We want
you to stay. This has been your first big test. You have
been worthy. It is what we hoped. Were any of you—
hurt?'

'Yes, a little,' said Anni, but made no move to exhibit
her own arm, and then: 'One of us is not alive now.'

It came as a slight shock to all. That one of the Clones

was dead. Naturally this would happen to them as to all
beings, as their tissues wore out, but it had only happened
two or three times before, except to the imperfect or damaged, and not all the Council knew of these earlier deaths.
'Which was it?' Mutumba asked, 'and how?'

'One of them had a gun hidden in his robe,' Anni said,
'one of these very old guns, the kind one sees in pictures.
He snatched it out and shot most of her brains away.
Otherwise we would have tried to keep her living. If it had
been heart or lungs. She was one of the oldest of us; her
experience had been with the space exploration group. She
had meant to be in the first galaxy crew. But that was not.'

'Her name?' Mutumba asked gently, 'we will remember
her,' and she wondered as others did, if the Clone girls
had loved.

'She was Ellen. Her advice was always good. She cared
for us who were younger. It was hard not to hate. We did
not kill that man although it would have been easy.'

'She must have been one of the first Clones,' said Ric,
who was standing beside Jussie. 'Do you remember what
her number was?'

'I remember. It was A Sixteen.'

Ric looked at Mutumba. It was beyond him not to. He
saw that it took several counted seconds to get down to the
memory centre, and then Mutumba was shaken as Jussie
had been shaken. She looked from side to side and her
grey-curled head seemed to quiver a little. Then she sat up
straighter than before. There were more questions, further
discussions. Jussie was joining in now she had taken and
absorbed the knowledge of what had happened and was
not allowing herself to imagine. In this context it would
have been interference: against the code.

One or two of the Council were still shocked and angry.

There had been nothing like this for a decade. It must not be. This had to be clearly expressed to the aggressors. If there was to be incentive in society there must also be punishment. At the least the communication media must force them to feel complete shame. Yet was this in terms of the code? Mutumba stood up and began to go round with the box and her blessing; she waited by each while the lighting-up was done. The box was ancient and ivory, carved with an intertwinement of forms, into which one could read what one would. She put her hand lightly on Jussie's shoulder. Only Ric had known that number. Stig might have known but had not noticed.

The sweetly dubious-smelling smoke of cannabis, the aggression dispeller, weaved and hung out of the lungs and about the heads of the Council. In this version, the best cannabis varieties of three continents had been blended. It was normally used on occasions when hatred, anger and prejudice might have crept into the minds of the Council. Now Jussie was able to remember the three days and nights of Elissa as something unforgettably lovely, gained from destroying time, a gift. She had felt young with Elissa; now she had returned to her own age. Yes, she was deeply sad, but the sadness was contained. She could think and make judgments. The flaxen Clone girl sat at Mutumba's feet; she inhaled deeply. In a little she was leaning back against the Convenor, not knowing exactly what she was doing, but relaxing, crying softly with no attempt to keep back the tears, while the image of Ellen's brains pouring bloodily out of her smashed skull, gradually dimmed. And Mutumba's thin, dark, hard-sinewed hands picked up her plaits, one after the other, and stroked their shining pale gold.

Now those they had to deal with were screened up, the

88

light brown, bony, puzzled faces, the questing eyes, and the young Clones with them, participating. In the screen picture too, cannabis was offered, but two of the negotiators refused. One was a tall, fierce woman, unlike anyone most of the Council had seen, wearing a long white cotton robe embroidered in heavy red. Even if communal aggression had been checked, personal aggression was still there. With a flash of bracelets, she knocked the smoke out of the hands of the Clone boy who had offered them. Gently he picked them up again. The smaller video screens for the absent Council members were all full now. The debate and negotiation began.

The sound of the language was strange and jarring, but each of the negotiators had a Clone doing instant translation, both ways. A smaller screen, visible to both parties, showed a few essential statistics which were being provided, as asked for, by the computers. Yet this seemed to make the negotiators on the screen uneasy; perhaps their new-found rationality had not reached that far. Collaborating with computers was a matter of practice, which they had not had. Their background seemed to be a very large tree with curious stones lying under it; beyond, just visible, was some kind of formal building and a glint of colour. Not one of the Council was quite clear on the species of the tree and the focus was on the people, not on possible inflorescences or leaf detail; some found this a little irritating.

As the arguments turned round, so often coming back to almost the same point, a few of the Council found themselves with other thoughts coming in, but knew this must not happen. Patience and concentration were essential. To let nothing else invade the mind while the persuasion was taking place. These were not stupid or ignorant people, but there had been a feed-in of anger and suspicion and nightmares, from a collective unconscious going far back in a history of alternate repressions and violent breaks of one kind or another.

Here, Ric knew what he was taking on. So, naturally, did Shanti, whose share of the same unconscious was not small. It was something immune to rational argument, but the Clones, by participating in it, had partly deflected and destroyed it. The negotiators were uneasy; two of them whispered, robes caught up over their mouths, then asked for time. Yes, said Mutumba, they could have all the time they needed.

One of the whisperers looked up and said, 'We can find you the ones who killed—your friends. If you wish.'

'We do not wish,' said Mutumba. 'Not now.'

CHAPTER TEN

LILAC sat there, her head hanging and her hands between her knees. She hadn't bothered about spray-on or scent. Her name bush was over, only a few scraps of purple left on the twigs. There were new lovely flowering bushes, fiery azaleas, magnolias like plates of cream; she wasn't interested, who wants to visit a flowering branch alone, alone? Gisela was gone and the gardens were empty. F Seventy One was gone too. Gisela had seen the Signs and rushed to tell; then it was all over. She had betrayed her child—to what? To Them. To the popu-curve and all the things in the picture screens and books. Going with the wave : what did that mean anyway? What did it have to do with Ninety or Seventy One? But then Seventy One wasn't really Gisela's child, only her Clone. The same with her own Ninety. What would it be like to have a really child with one's own genes? But that would mean—before one could do it—this thing with a man—no, one couldn't! Even to think of it made her a little queasy about the stomach.

And yet her own Mum must have—with her Dad. Ever so long ago before people knew. But they can't have liked it. Well, one couldn't. Or could one have long ago? There were some of the old books she had read. Shakespeare. But of course she knew that Romeo was just as much a girl as

Juliet. It was only that in those cruel times there had to be
this pretence. And anyhow with two haphazard hetero-
sexuals nobody could tell how the genes would work out.
That was the sin of meiosis, the upsetting of reason and
planning, re-shuffling the chromosomes just anyhow! After
all, supposing her gene mixture from Mum and Dad had
made her thin and small hipped, then they wouldn't have
chosen her as a Clone mum. Or if it had made her too
bright so that she wouldn't—well, wouldn't have been so
happy with all she was told.

But she wasn't happy now. She kept watching Ninety,
the way he was building, not like the others. And she kept
looking out for a watcher or carer who might see the Signs.
If any of them came near she went down on her knees
beside the children and managed to knock down the tower
or the house or whatever it was, or upset the slot box or
start them on a race or bounce a ball at them. He could
hold a colour blob and mark with it; this was a Sign. She
knew, she knew! Oh, it had been fun dodging with Gisela
helping, so shocked but could she say so? Fun shocking
Gisela, making her quiver and then slapping her and getting her down and rolling her and turning tears into giggles
and—nothing was fun now, only she had to pretend. And
to guard Ninety.

She looked round. There was one of the watchers
coming, Ragmi. And Ninety was making a pattern of flowers. A definite pattern. She picked him up, put him on her
shoulders, scuffed the pattern with her feet and called to
the others to chase them. Usually he enjoyed this and held
on tight—the feel of his arms soft on her neck, strong little
fingers on her cheeks, ears, nose. But he didn't want it—
screamed—and of course Ragmi noticed and came over
and asked what he had been doing.

'You know, Lilac,' she said, 'I'm hoping he'll show the Signs any day now. It's time.' But had Ragmi guessed? Had she seen something he was doing? Or had one of the other Mums? If only she could find another friend, a lover who would help and hide. But, as it was, she had to guard him all the time against one of Them noticing too. One had to be so clever, much cleverer than she was. Supposing while she was asleep he started playing and someone came in—was it worth it? She hadn't thought it out, only knew she was against Them and she wanted so much to be able to go on loving Ninety and not to betray him, but they got suspicious, they'd watch all the time—and he, they'd take him—and she'd be punished. Somehow. She knew that. It had been fun to defy them—with Gisela—but not now. Nothing was fun.

She put him down again by the sand and the little pond. There were a lot of other Mums there and she could forget for a bit. None of the special Signs toys anywhere. Let's play a game, a brain twister, one of the new games, a computer room girl like me ought to beat the rest!

Jussie came over, looking as kind as she always did somehow, but she asked Lilac to bring Ninety along. So she picked him up, hugging him tight all over because she could feel it was the end and then they were in a room with the Sign toys and it was too late. Too late. 'What made you do it, Lilac?' asked Jussie. Lilac looked all round and there was no help—she'd got to answer. Quietly Jussie handed her a smoke; she shook her head. 'It's not doped,' said Jussie. 'Only the usual; we don't want to talk in a state of tension, do we?'

'I'll do what I'm told,' Lilac muttered, and took the smoke, realizing that she'd hardly ever wanted one in the gardens, least of all when Gisela was there. She inhaled

but, not yet feeling the soothing of the cannabis, said dully:
'You've taken him.'

'For his strengthening,' said Jussie. 'You don't really
want him to miss being one of the future, do you? You
know, Lilac, he may be one of the Council when people like
me are dead and gone.'

Lilac didn't answer. That was the kind of tricking thing
They said. At last she asked: 'What are you going to do to
me?'

'Understand you, I hope,' said Jussie, and then con-
versationally: 'You know, Lilac, this is the first time that
any of the Clone Mums have hidden the Signs. Most are
so proud. They want theirs to be first. But you didn't.
Why?'

'Taking him away,' said Lilac, low through the smoke.
'Hurting him, mine. Mine.'

'You understood. You accepted. You accepted in joy
that you had been lent something of Him. From the beginning you knew and accepted. This is how after the loan has
been returned you will be crowned and loved and admired.
You are taking in and sheltering Him and Her in the very
deeps of your bodies.' Now Jussie was repeating the words
and phrases which had been used early on in the books, in
the pictures, in the singing: Them. Lilac felt herself being
lulled, not by the cannabis which barely affected her, but
by the words, the overtones, all she had agreed on so joyfully
and been made happy by in the first months of her pregnancy. She began to mutter about it, unwilling to explain
and yet knowing she must. And Jussie listened. Yes, it was
true, she had felt herself chosen, privileged; her friends when
she videoed them were admiring, loving. Yes, even in the
delivery room while she was putting her ante-natal exercises into practice, the thoughts that had been given her

94

with the exercises buoyed her up. Naturally the Clone Mums were carefully looked after: effort was expected, discomfort even, but no pain.

And then she had begun reading the books and thinking about the world as it was for Her and Him, but not just about how He and She had changed it all, which was what the books were supposed to make you understand, but about what it was they'd fought against. And then as she went on reading it began to seem as if the same thing was still happening. Not quite the same, but—she looked quickly at Jussie, but Jussie still looked tired. She hadn't known she was going to think like that through reading the books, it had surprised her. But there it was. The words stared at her. The police state. But not police any longer: instead watchers and carers. Jussie. And who was suffering? Not so much ordinary people who had suffered in the police states in the old days and been bullied and unhappy and had lost their identity. No, now it was the baby Clones and the Clone mums who must fight for them. The suffering was going on, pinpointed this way. But her Ninety, her own child, must get the chance to grow up different, to be always happy and loved, to make the music of perpetual happiness. Somehow. That was what she was saving him for. His genes of goodness must be used in love and not in stress. But nobody else understood. Not soft lovely Gisela, the sun in her hair, who had let her own baby go. And now she herself had been defeated.

'It couldn't have gone on,' Jussie said. 'Could it, Lilac? You might have hidden it another month perhaps, not longer. Surely you understood that?'

'He was mine,' said Lilac. 'Fed on my milk. My little mammal. My own.'

'But—' said Jussie patiently, 'he was only lent to you

95

and you know that, Lilac. You know it is wrong for one person to assert ownership over another, even a lover, but most of all over a little child. A little Clone.'

'If I could have saved him—it wouldn't have been wrong.'

'I wonder, Lilac,' said Jussie very patiently, 'if you weren't a little jealous? Didn't you wish that your own genes were there? We all know we are unworthy but sometimes we can't help our thoughts and feelings. Did that happen to you?'

But Lilac didn't answer. She wanted desperately to get it over, to go away—but would she be allowed? To get to some place where she could forget. Not think about Ninety—they won't have started doing anything, not yet— or will they? She stood up; it was a pleasant living space, she supposed. There was a window looking out on to the gardens, a real window. Trees. Flowers. She didn't want to see them. There were the toys. They had seen as soon as he began to play with the slot boxes. She gave them a hard kick. She and Jussie were alone there. Jussie had seen but she had not moved. She didn't look angry or even sad. She wore a green spray-on with a bit of deep red, plainer than most. Why? Her face was lined, barely made up, but she had perhaps been beautiful once. Her eyes were flecked brown, heterozygous eyes, curiously kind; people's eye intentions are hard to hide. There was a small scar on her cheek bone, bluish, hardly a blemish, a point of interest. Lilac found herself staring but didn't care. Jussie said: 'It was a mine explosion. My first pit, a very early experience, I was not yet in charge. I suppose the scar could have been taken away; but perhaps one should allow one's life and one's work to mark one. You've been in computers, haven't you? Do you want to go back?'

Was this some kind of trap? Lilac came close to Jussie and looked at her hard, searching, and suddenly not wondering if Jussie was going to punish her, but instead who exactly Jussie was and what genes were mixed in her. She'd heard somewhere that Jussie had been a mining engineer but it hadn't meant anything till she saw the scar. And now Jussie was asking apparently, did she want to change her own life. But— 'You're going to punish me,' she said, 'for what I tried to do. I want to know what it will be. I must know!'

Jussie said : 'But you are being punished. You are feeling it.'

So this was it, defeat, fear, utter resentment. 'But Ninety—' she said, '—my baby, who did nothing to be punished for!'

'Except being born a Clone,' said Jussie, leaning forward, so close that Lilac could have touched the scar. 'Able to take what comes to him and make it into strength. Look, Lilac, we are very careful of them. They are very precious. We don't damage them. The strengthening sounds worse that it is because it would be bad for any who were not worthy of it. It is hard on them, it must be; it is something they don't want to talk about when it is over, even to one another. But it seems to be necessary at one stage or another and it is thought that the best way for them is to concentrate it in their early years so that it becomes absorbed and they can grow out of it into deeper understanding. Do you see at all, Lilac?'

'But what would happen if they were allowed to grow up with those genes and without this—strengthening?'

'We don't know,' said Jussie. 'Except that the world isn't ready for them, not yet. And once there are enough of them we're going to start again on space exploration.

We can't have ordinary people like ourselves doing it; we aren't fit; we'd be too frightened to make contact, supposing there is other life in space, as we are increasingly certain there must be. But for that they will need to have been strengthened. Maybe your Ninety will be one of them.'

'But I shan't know.'

'Perhaps you will. Perhaps you will be there to see his rocket leave, as an honoured guest. That depends on you. Think again about the computers. Certainly you could go back. You'd be admired as a Clone Mum. Oh, yes! Gisela would screen you up. Nothing would be said—about this. You wouldn't need to say anything to Gisela and she wouldn't dare say anything to you.'

Gisela. Golden soft Gisela whom she had loved in the gardens which were at the far side of that window. But she had turned her back on it. And on her own Mum. And free rides in the recreation spaces and all that. 'Or else?' she asked.

'Well, there is some interesting research going on. You seem able to have learnt to draw inferences from books. You might be still better at drawing them from experimental data. There is by now an extensive set of data on the Clones. It has to be analysed in various ways. There is— and I think this would interest you—some evidence of non-chromosomal maternal influence from the cell material.'

'After my chromosomes were knocked out? I mean anyone's?' She was still watching Jussie, watching for the catch.

'The lab work is being done in the other hemisphere. A mega-city something like this. If you were giving it a try you could see them at work and look at the data this side. You could go back to your old living space or an equivalent and work from there. You could be with your friends.

You could be admired and taken on interesting journeys. But if you were to find the work deeply interesting you would be doing better to go over there. However, apart from this, there is some rather unexpected material about other influences on the Clones. It is not merely the physical difference between one uterus and another, but there is also considerable interchange of fluids between the foetus and its host.'

'Yes,' said Lilac guardedly. It was what she had been aware of, even without knowing the anatomical detail.

'Also,' said Jussie, 'there is some difference in maternal influence during the first two years. The watchers and carers minimize this. But it exists. Again, most of the statistical data are in the Australian centre.'

Lilac looked down at the broken toy. 'Is this a punishment?' she said suddenly.

Jussie shook her head. 'No. Nor is it a reward. But you seem to have certain abilities which should be used. And which you would enjoy using.'

'Do you think so?' said Lilac. 'Oh, Jussie, do you really think so?' Jussie nodded. 'Then—then I'd rather go where I can take it on. Let me have the data and I'll start. I'd like to go to the other hemisphere. I've never actually done lab work but I think I could. I'm sure I could do the statistical work!'

She was flushed, excited and exciting. Was it for this that soft Gisela had loved her? 'All right,' said Jussie. And then added: 'Your computer programming practice will be useful, but you will have to learn to look at the data properly before you go to Australia. You will stay here for the moment. I might be able to find time to help you myself.'

CHAPTER ELEVEN

THE Outer Mongolian expedition were all getting rather
tired, especially Miryam, who was older than the other
three. Few people were accustomed to long walks on rough
ground and this was the only way to keep a close, botanical
look for what she was after. In cities, yes. Even on the walkways those in a hurry could use their legs rather than watch
the pictures as they went by, and there was some cycling,
though, of course, in cities, petrol and diesel fumes had
long been banned, not that there was much in the way of
oil reserves left. Other forms of energy were mostly unsuitable for vehicles, which, anyhow, usually led to aggression
by the users, however much they tried to guard against it.
But town walking did not get anyone used to walking on
untreated earth, cold in the early morning, but hot and
crumbling by midday.

Here in the food fields they had been taken over tracks
in what was called an idjeep, dirty and smelly, using some
crude local oil fuel, but good fun; it carried some of their
necessary lab equipment; to save bumping some of it had
been loaded down on genuine animal skins. Miryam and
Cheng had both flinched a little when they touched them
and realized what they were, and had warned the other
two, who were younger and had not been on an expedition

before; they might have made some sort of protest, not only
useless, but entirely unintelligible to the people they were
living among. But by now they were all getting used to
that kind of thing, even to the local feasts where they had
to eat animal protein, cooked certainly, but making one
sickeningly aware of its origin, as well as various milk
products. Some of the latter were quite acceptable and even
palatable. Cheng, who had been in this part of the world
before and whose child-language had much in common
with that of Mongolia, knew rather too much about their
origins, but Toto in particular had taken to the curds
which seemed to be part of every meal. There was an alco-
holic drink which they made out of one of the berries : it
was quite pleasant and all the expedition tried it. But it
had something of a hangover, and they could not afford
to be at all disabled.

Now on the edges of the food fields there was much of
great botanical interest; but so far nothing in the way of
early triticums. They had been painstakingly eliminated
early on, weeded out by women with broad, bread-brown
faces, slightly slit-eyed, wearing enormous silver and tur-
quoise earrings and necklaces and swinging heavy skirts
of all too genuine wool. At one camp the women, discovering that Miryam and Tsing-Lo were the same sex as themselves, had insisted on dressing them up, and the animal
smell was such that both had found it difficult to smile
and use the praise words which Cheng, who was a brilliant
interpreter, had found for them. Embarrassingly, the local
women had praised Miryam's breasts which were clearly
somewhat maternal and had pitied Tsing-Lo; they had
gone so far as offering her a man to make her grow. Poor
Tsing-Lo had almost fainted. Cheng had come to the rescue
by saying that he was Tsing-Lo's man. Tota had then been

allocated to Miryam. It had all been rather funny in a way.

Ulan Bator had been almost under control population-wise, though some of the methods were very unpleasant, especially the whipping of deviants by non-deviants. As deviant women were often not recognized until late pregnancy this resulted in the nastiest kind of aggression; there were occasional public castrations to the sound of drums. The Clones whom they had met at that first opera-plus performance had been deeply upset, even to the point of questioning the whole popu-policy. They and the expedition had videoed back to the nearest Council group at Honan, not that much could be expected at once. It would be a matter of skilled participation and understanding before the people who seemed to enjoy the whippings and castrations, not quite aggressively, but simply as a show, and had a well developed spy system, could have their minds cleaned enough to live by the Code. But even in Ulan Bator there were quite a lot of children among the rich—and it was a place where there were still dreadful inequalities, apparently acceptable—and some categories, for instance, actors, racing camel riders and girl ski champions, seemed to be immune from control. In a sense this seemed logical since drama, camel racing and ski contests were the main aggression substitutes for this national group.

But out here in the food fields the popu-policy might never have existed. The expedition had been prepared for this. After all, it was only working adequately in the advanced mega-cities where the reasons for it were so overwhelming and where it had been formulated earliest through closely controlled mass media. It had never been enforced out here. World government was recognized but not yet world policy. The expedition discussed occasionally the probable result of world population being added to almost entirely among the less technically advanced peoples, but saw nothing against it. After all, they were *homo faber* and might well in the long run provide men and women of original genius and insight. A Her or a Him one day? Well, anything was possible and seemed more so when they talked about it in the long cut-off evenings. Yet the large families who could not possibly all make a living out on the food fields, did contribute to the surplus population of Ulan Bator and indeed of other large cities. Once there, popu-policy would begin to work on them, as well as much else. However even here far out there was a general knowledge and interest in Him and Her and it was through this that policies would gradually work. It was disconcerting all the same to be shown reverently a picture of Him, large, heavily-bearded—and white. 'He brings gifts in the middle of winter,' said one of the older women, 'to help us over the hard times. He gave us the new waters.'

'Yes, he helps us,' said the others.

'Indeed yes,' said the expedition solemnly, glancing at one another.

'Grandfather Frost,' whispered Cheng, 'or possibly Marx.'

These little groups of mud-brick and felt houses seemed temporary, quite unplanned, as though people who had been wandering at horse pace or camel pace had dismounted and simply not moved on. There would be a well, some of the favourite vegetables grown rather haphazard, perhaps a few fruit trees. Rather shockingly, they grew tobacco, for their own use of course; the expedition hated to think what their lungs must be like.

It wasn't always easy to tell what was wild and what more or less cultivated. The climatic changes and the raising of the water table by the beautiful new lakes had altered the flora considerably. If they wanted to work in the food fields the people of these family villages could and mostly did, but the authorities still left them grazing grounds, though goats were forbidden. One still saw the occasional yak, though most had been replaced by better milking cattle. Time enough to tidy up these loose ends; meanwhile, they were not dangerous, except perhaps to themselves; the infant death rate, for instance, was practically unchanged. Miryam, almost involuntarily, found herself doing a bit of primitive medical work.

At the edges of the wheat fields there would be a crop of hybrids of the triticums, mostly sterile and almost all known and noted already. What Miryam hoped for was one little patch somewhere kept and sown year after year from an old variety, perhaps by one isolated family. So she looked round the settlements and on small hilly patches and it was here she came on something that was not a wheat or wheat grass, but a sight that equally fixed her—a grove of little almond trees with the yellow spot.

It was only too easy to recognize. She cut off a branch. Yes, it was the virus and a good deal worse than anything she had seen with Carlo. Two of the women watching her came close, pulled her by the hand and took her to an apple tree equally diseased. Within two or three days she and the others had seen dozens of rosaceae; pyrus, prunus, rubus, the lot, all infected, some mildly, others badly. A few trees and shrubs seemed to be quite dead. On all, the fruit was distorted, though the almond kernels seemed to survive for one year at least. When they discovered what she was looking for there was plenty of local information and Cheng was kept busy interpreting. The trees which had died of viral infection all had a specially unpleasant look; the last leaves seemed to be left hanging blackly at a curious angle.

Was it possible then, that once again Central Asia was the source of yet another invasion?

The expedition was in touch of course, but not by video, and long range communication still had its difficulties. They asked for a helicopter to come for specimens and the report, and this duly happened. People were quite used to the spraying and fertilizing helis, but had never seen one close and had their own ideas about them. After it had left, loaded with specimens and report capsules, there was a lot of laughter and cry-outs on the local strings and percussion. The expedition had noted that, though the scattered villagers had transistors and sometimes listened to songs, they didn't bother with them much but preferred making their own. This seemed altogether a good thing, averting the identity crisis, but made it harder to get policies across.

That evening there was a helicopter song and dance. Cheng translated, giggling to himself sometimes. 'It seems that He sent it,' said Cheng, 'out of the high heavens.'

'That's half true,' Tsing-Lo said.

'But listen how it was done—' They were all laughing now, even if it was a little bit shocking too. '—and you, Miryam, will cure the trees. Next year there will be plenty of fruit, almonds, plums, pears—they're going through the different names, I'll make a list, there's a different drum note to each—oh yes, and there'll be plenty of babies too!'

But the expedition had almost stopped being embarrassed. They were aware that they had only been thrown back to an earlier bit of human history when local popucurves might go down in sudden disastrous ways, which had to be guarded against. It did not, of course, affect them personally. Toto still flirted with Cheng, and Tsing-Lo had somehow not realized that Miryam was a deviant and had supposed that her somewhat heavy breasts and her intelligent interest in and handling of the local babies, with their rather disgusting smell of sour milk and urine and un- washed woollen blankets, was the result of having been a Clone Mum. So she did a bit of normal sidling up and caressing which Miryam tried to respond to in a respect- able way. She must not, of course, speak of her colleague the cytologist with more than ordinary friendliness. In fact she overdid it and Tsing-Lo gently blamed her for finding Carlo distasteful merely because he was a man.

The expedition had now a double aim. They had all been told about the virus, but as the original purpose had been the search for early wheats and wheat-grasses they had not been so intently on the lookout as Miryam had been. Now however they were alerted. They spread out, trying to find how far the locus of infection was spread. The next helicopter had some fresh instructions including a recorded message from Carlo. His voice. But of course not a word about the children nor, for that matter, to herself as a person. Well, that was how things were. Meanwhile Toto had found what seemed like a possible early wheat; Miryam did not recognize it and was delighted. They harvested the clump carefully by hand; the local people looked on and laughed. 'We are mad,' said Cheng, 'but not bad.' Soon after Tsing-Lo found another, definitely dwarf- form with peculiar bracts.

Over the days their walking muscles got into trim; they went further and had occasion to observe the smaller fauna of which there were quite a lot. They had several times been offered fur and feathers which were heart-rendingly beautiful. Tentatively Cheng spoke once in a crowded, nicotine-smoke filled hut, of the unity of nature, hoping that it might abate some of this murder. But the only response came from a very old man, half asleep in the corner, who turned out to have been a Buddhist teacher in the old days. There were still ideas in common although he dated back before the wave. If it could be said that it had ever reached this far.

Then one day a group of locals were discussing something excitedly and finally came to the expedition. 'They ask us to come,' said Cheng. They were all rather tired and Tsing-Lo and Toto were both hunched over the microscopes; it wasn't too easy to get the light right, or indeed much else, for people used to working in lab conditions. So it was decided that they needn't come.

'They say it is something good,' said Cheng. 'Something has come back from death.' He added with distaste and a certain degree of fear, 'I hope we are not running into something from an old religion. They are using somewhat formal words.'

'I don't think so,' Miryam said. 'They haven't that look.' But she too was a little uneasy and wondered where they were going and why. It was a longish walk away.

And then the locals separated out and they saw what it was. Two little dead almond trees, killed by the virus. But not dead. All along the branches they were budding, pushing out green tips—and at this time of year. Miryam met the eyes of the senior man, dark eyes, hemmed in and slanted by the epicanthic fold, but good and kind even though some harmless beautiful bird had been killed for the feathers which were wound round his cap. She took his hand and he knelt and kissed the ground, pulling her down with him. All knelt, even at last Cheng, much embarrassed but not wanting to be conspicuous.

CHAPTER TWELVE

'NEED you go yet?' Ric asked. He had tried to speak lightly but it was no good. Pain had come into his voice and he knew it was unpleasant: wanting instead of loving. How could Bobbi possibly like this kind of voice? Yes, he would care dutifully but there was a difference between caring and active love. If Bobbi saw it as a necessary part of caring he would allow himself to touch and be touched. He would perhaps allow—anything. But none of that was enough.

'I'll come back, sure,' muttered Bobbi uncomfortably. And did he, Ric asked himself, have another Clone boy whom he loved, naturally so much worthier than all that Ric could ever be? How beautiful the loves and sports of the Clone boys, the young Spartiates! Yes, yes, he must not keep Bobbi back. 'Wish you didn't look so cast down,' said Bobbi. 'Look, man, I liked your music poem. You mustn't think I was criticizing. Me, I don't make sense about poems, not yet, not beyond what you've taught me. Maybe I will one day. Ah, Ric, isn't there anything I can do for you?'

And suppose I began to answer truthfully what would happen. What indeed? 'Yes,' said Ric. 'There is. Would you take your shirt off?'

'Why, yes,' said Bobbi, puzzled. But surely he under-stood? Surely he'd had feelings? Slowly he unbuttoned the cotton shirt and pulled it over his head and stood, his brown chest heaving a little, quite smooth as His must have been. Oh, if one could have seen Him as a young man!

For a long moment Ric looked and looked. His hand crept out. He saw himself give one quick strong tug at the blue jeans. No. 'It's strange to think He must have looked like you,' he said. 'Just like.'

'Why, sure,' said Bobbi. 'That's bound to be, Ric. Stands to reason. But the way I see it, well, it makes us Clones a bit too alike, a bit dull, all having the same genes.' He moved slightly away, picked up a book at random and put it in the scanner upside down.

Displacement activity. No, one mustn't treat one of the Clones this way. 'Well,' said Ric brightly, 'I don't find you dull but I ought to be doing some work. We've a Council meeting tomorrow and rather a lot of data to get through. Come over any time, Bobbi. Here's your shirt.' He handed it back: warm from his body, a little crumpled, the way genuine cotton gets.

'Well, thanks a lot, Ric. You're fine now? Yes, of course you are.' He ducked into the shirt and smiled fleetingly and was away. There was a whole night to get through. Curious the things one didn't know about Him, in spite of all that had been written and pictured. If one did, one could prob-ably understand the behaviour of the Clones. But so much was left out. The popu-policy had been thought out before His time but did we know how much He had been touched by it? No record. Or She? Yes, She had been one of the organizers even before Her immense contribution had become plain. But they were an earlier generation. Had

They been deeply affected from birth as later generations were? One did not like even to ask oneself this, but was it possible that either or both of Them had at one time at least had faint hetero-sexual yearnings? Yet even if this had been so their Clones, their representatives today, had gone through normal education and social conditioning. Anything else was unthinkable.

And yet he kept on thinking it. And was quite unable to get to sleep and wondered how he could be cared for, what he could say to the carer. He could not possibly mention his doubts and yet, the more he thought about them, the more urgent and complex it all became. If one could imagine the unimaginable, as he was doing, the union of two Clones, how would it be? The result would not necessarily be a combination of two kinds of excellence. He knew enough genetics to realize this. And then? And if that was conceivably why Bobbi had left him?

He got up and walked about his room, turned the landscape screen on and then off. He looked at the quiet little statue in the *toko-no-ma* and suddenly hated it. Somehow he wasn't managing to turn his mind on to any other of his loves; he had pictures of them all, but when he put them onto the screen, nothing about them came true; none of them, it seemed, had ever quite met his deepest needs, whatever he had thought at the time. He took a smoke but it had a bad effect. It made him see Bobbi. No use. He had no other of the possibly addictive drugs. Council members did not use alcohol, nicotine or any of the hallucinogens; they were not forbidden, but it was completely out of social character.

What then? Should he video someone? Stig? No, there was only one whose face he wanted to call up. It was ill thought of for the Council members to take sleeping pills but worse to come to a Council meeting in an impaired state. And he should have been thinking about the rather odd way his special computer had put together Stig's worries, comparing them with other data which it had in its immense poetic memory. Sometimes he felt too small and unworthy to deal with his computer although he had spent so much time developing and further developing it, standing over the engineers, insisting on elegance and economy of output and feeding it with facts and questions both on history and on current events. He was sometimes almost afraid of its complexities; perhaps it was because of this that he so much needed Bobbi's innocence. So much. So much. A sleeping pill? Well, it was his own responsibility. At last he slept.

After the last meeting Mutumba had asked Anni to come back with her and share her living space for a few days. No need for her to go back to the aggression point if things went on all right over there, as it appeared they were doing. It would give her arm a chance of healing on its own through rest. Anni had said yes, indeed she would come and yes, she would tell Mutumba all about Ellen; it was good that the Council cared so much for the Clones. There was just room for her to sleep comfortably in Mutumba's living space. Mutumba herself had learned to ration herself on sleep, allowing herself three periods of dream and three of deep unconsciousness. After this the little electrodes woke her; she was quite used to them. Only a few people had taken advantage of this method; it needed habits of discipline as well as some scientific sense, but Mutumba had both.

Anni was still asleep. Mutumba watched her. Her own lovely baby would have been like this. Ellen. She had never known the name. At that time no Clone Mum was told.

Ellen would have been a little older, that was all, but with the same long fair plaits. Otherwise of course she would be exactly alike; there was no genetic difference and little of experience. Perhaps the strengthening techniques were more developed in Anni's time: less tough in some ways but possibly more in others. It would not have made Ellen's cheeks and lips unlike Anni's, as both were like Hers. All had the same serious look, the pale complexion and thin nose; all were slightly but not disablingly myopic. These Shetland copies who had never seen the voes and cliffs except in screen pictures, had never heard the real birds screaming above the waves! Bonxies and Arctic terns— Mutumba had seen them in real life circling deafeningly round her head.

Anni half opened blue eyes, murmured 'Mum'. Then woke fully and saw Mutumba and blushed. 'I had a dream,' she said apologizing, but smiling at the same time.

'Did you ever see your Mum?' Mutumba asked.

Anni shook her head. 'None of my lot ever saw our Mums. Were you—' What daring to the Convener of the Council! '—were you ever a Clone Mum?'

'Yes, I was,' Mutumba said.

'Then perhaps—you could have been my real Mum!'

'Yes, Anni darling, I could have been.' She stooped over and stroked the smooth pale gold head. 'My dear Anni,' she said.

There was now one Council meeting after another with different groups coming in. Few of the members had time for any of their work. Jussie, who had long given it up, found herself wishing for the comparative quiet of being a top mining engineer in those very deep Antarctic pits where extreme heat and extreme cold met at either end of the lift shaft. Just now she was not even visiting her Clone

Mums but merely getting reports from the watchers and carers. She had not seen Lilac again, but oddly, found herself wondering how she was getting on with her new work. And again Andrei had to leave his huge public health project in the difficult area of the Aral Sea where pollution, following an altered water level, had been allowed to go too far. Andrei disliked not being in constant touch, but he could not be away from the Council now.

Most of the business was of course about the aggression, not merely the details of the negotiations and safeguards, but the insistence on genuinely accepted world government balanced by as much freedom of thought, custom and identity as was compatible. A very old problem, and the computer memories brought out all the solutions and mistakes and the few successes. This time surely it could work! But also there must be a digging down into the nature of this particular aggression, where it had sprung from and why it had suddenly gathered force: how it should have been monitored and why it had not been. The negotiators had finally given in Elissa's wrist recorder with the full notes. It appeared to be only a little damaged although it was stained with something which Mutumba knew was Elissa's blood. She had gone on recording almost to the end.

But there were other uneasinesses. One of the Council members, normally rather taciturn, had videoed from Mexico about a certain patchiness in the wheat crop: Mexico, the first source of the new cereals away back in the twentieth century. They had all looked at the picture. Yes, even the least informed had understood at once. No, it did not appear to be a virus. No, nor any type of fungal infection. Yes, the crops had all been treated exactly the same; there had been no mistake on soil analysis. Yes, it could be extremely serious. Yes, he had contacted the Professorials. The one he would have liked appeared to be in Central Asia and out of touch, but it appeared that he also was anxious about the wheats from a somewhat different angle. Cytological. She could be on the right track. If anything went wrong with the cereals. The maize? That seemed to be okay, so far. Had he got any of the Clones experiencing with him? Yes—and here he allowed himself a slight smile—there was young Chuck. Well, no doubt something would come of it all. Meanwhile they had better look out. It would be as well to have monitoring flights over all the food fields. Yes, all, even Australia. And including though there was no report of anything wrong with the sorghum and millet where it was still grown. He would see to it that all personnel were instructed on what to look out for.

So it was arranged. Some of the Clones would certainly want to go and might have some good ideas. It was beginning to look as though all food fields must be given a once over, not only the wheat. Not only the cereals, even, legumes. As yet. People who worked in them all the time might not recognize the very slow unevenness or disturbance of balance or might put it down to a mistake over fertilizers or irrigation. Like so many other revolutions, the green revolution of the twentieth century, welcome at the time, had been having some rather unforeseen long term results.

There were other more routine matters which had to be settled, some in the nature of city planning and cleaning, with reports on methods and comments by the computers, but less attention than usual was being paid to them. Comments by the Councillors indicated that unusual trains of thought had been set in motion. Mutumba lifted her head. 'Friends,' she said, 'I may be all wrong but it seems to me that we're all wanting to think fresh. Maybe it's a wave. Could be. In our time. We've worked, all of us.'

Stig was the one who answered. 'If we could see—for ourselves. Beyond the wars. It's been a long haul. And this catching us at the end. Elissa. Through her, us. And the others. We've got this last aggression contained : right. But there's no telling what's going on at the roots, there or perhaps elsewhere.'

'I am sadly disappointed in the computers,' said Shanti precisely. Her English had a studied quality, though sometimes odd.

'They're only an extension of our brains and our parents' brains,' said Andrei. 'We can't expect too much of them.'

'What they give us is logic and shape,' said Ric. 'They take away the passion that hinders us.'

'But about the wheats,' said Jussie. 'I ask myself if this result could have been been foreseen earlier. Well, at least we have this expedition in Central Asia looking for varieties which can be built on again. Supposing there is some kind of catastrophe.'

'It certainly was foreseen earlier,' said Ric, 'in the second half of the twentieth century, to be exact. There was even what they then called a novel written about it—'

'But not,' said Stig, 'by a computer.'

CHAPTER THIRTEEN

'MAY I come in?' Anni said at the door of Mutumba's living space. She stood there and smiled and Mutumba felt a curious leap of affection towards her. She had been down with her old Clone group at one of the recreation spaces. Fair enough, the young Clones were all passionately hard workers; it was good for them to play games, swim and dive, leap the lights, devise shadow plays, make things to give to one another, watch acrobatics and conjurers and other highly-skilled manual performers, or take part in one of a dozen creative and delightful activities. Without being aware of it they would be influencing other people in recreation spaces, probably leading them, and getting rid of aggression in competitive games, serious—yet laughable. Anni was looking happier, less strained; that was good. But why had she bothered to come all this way herself instead of videoing?

'If you were really my Mum,' said Anni, 'I could talk to you about anything and you wouldn't mind?'

'That's right,' said Mutumba and wondered sharply what was coming and waited for it.

'I accept the popu-policy of course,' said Anni and then seemed not to know how to go on. She scuffed with her foot and abruptly asked: 'How do we know about Her—

Her that I'm part of? Did She—did She ever—think people were beautiful? Think it suddenly?'

'Oddly enough there's evidence for that,' Mutumba said, and patted the couch beside her so that Anni would sit down and relax. 'In India when she was still at the mission hospital. Well, it seems there were patients waiting and they were not beautiful. Not to others, not to anyone just ordinary. They were—well, some of them were just patients who hadn't taken what was offered them, family planning pills for instance. Do you get what I mean?' Anni nodded with a little shiver. 'And sometimes plain ugly with illnesses and bad feeding and maybe accidents that hadn't been looked after. A doctor is always kind, she has empathy; but She found them beautiful. She said so out loud. It was a surprise to some, so they write, because she was tough too. Tough as you know to be tough, Anni.'

'Only they weren't beautiful the way people are now,' said Anni.

'Maybe not. Were these people just now in the recreation space looking beautiful to you?'

Anni nodded. 'Some of them.'

'Was it—which? the high-diving girls? The cleave of the air? I always like to see them.'

But Anni shook her head. 'No. Can I tell you? I thought all of a sudden—that *men* were beautiful.'

'So they are. So they sure are if they're good. It shines through.' Mutumba was trying to speak very calmly.

'It didn't seem like that to me. It was more like—fruit. If you hadn't had any for a long time.'

'Was it men? Or one man?'

'It was—one of my Clone group. A little younger than me. Catching one of the light balls. So beautiful.' Anni was looking in front of her, revisualizing, and did not notice that Mutumba had relaxed a very little at the knowledge that it was at least another Clone. Then suddenly she turned and questioned with big eyes. 'Am I a deviant?'

'This is how deviants feel, my dear Anni,' said Mutumba.

'But how can I be?' She was frightened now and this, thought Mutumba, was not right. Perhaps Anni had never been really frightened before, not in this way.

'Could be the influence of the maternal cytoplasm,' said Mutumba, calmly, 'or other fluids. For example, there could be hormones in the placenta. Circulating through, having their effect. Though we try to check on this.' There were records, of course, she could find out in what womb this stranger had nested. She had not already done so because—well, because she wanted to think of herself as Anni's Mum.

'But we're all alike!' said Anni.

'Not as alike as you think,' said Mutumba quickly, 'nor as alike as you look. Genetically you're all the same. Right. You couldn't have dark hair or red hair nor yet brown hair, or anything but blue eyes. You couldn't be long-sighted. You couldn't be diabetic, for instance. What's more, you all have the same finger and thumb whorls. Same for the boys. But the babies don't get one another mixed; they know. You've only got to watch. So if you're the least bit deviant, Anni, don't go thinking your sisters will be. It's some other influence.'

'But am I? Am I? I know it's wrong!'

'I wouldn't say it was wrong. It's not against the code. There are good people who are deviants.' She had one arm round Anni, who was shaking with sobs.

'Can there be? Could there be a Council member who was a deviant? Please—please tell me!'

Mutumba said nothing for a long minute and then she spoke slowly and deliberately. 'Why, yes. The Council's a very big body. Not all of them were at the meeting you saw. Not even counting the ones who participated through the screen. A few have had deviant years early on and then got past it. That can happen.' Mutumba thought back. 'I remember two who had sudden deviant feelings for one another. Both tried to get over it. They kept it under control, painfully I'm afraid. Then I got to know. You see, Anni, I get to know plenty; that way I don't get worried. I told those cats to go ahead, not hurt one another, not upset other people. I didn't want to lose them, see? They went ahead. Then they got over it, stayed friends. That can happen, Anni.'

'I didn't know.'

'Human beings are about the most variable animal there is. One gets to understand. Could be there's a deviant or two on the Council now. In fact—yes. We don't spy on one another.'

But Anni was intent on her own problem. 'Should I try to get over this? Not to give way?'

'Would that be difficult, Anni?'

'Yes,' she said. 'Very difficult. I would have to force myself not to see this beautiful man : this man who seems to me to be beautiful.'

'Force,' said Mutumba slowly. And then, ' And this beautiful man of yours? Does he think you are beautiful, Anni?'

'Yes,' said Anni, 'I am sure of that. It was when I was looking at him he looked back at me. Then we spoke.' She frowned. 'What I am saying is stupid and not how it was. How it is. I find it hard to find words for something which is so far from anything which I supposed I might experience. I am finding it full of pain since the words I would want to use are the words I would use to another woman if that were to come my way. It is a little strange perhaps that it has not done so. I had hoped it would.'

'Could be,' said Mutumba, 'that your hormone balance made that unlikely and this likely. You've done nothing wrong.'

'I said I would see him,' said Anni, 'but instead you can keep me here.' She was breathing quick and hard. 'You are my Mum, you know, or almost, and I have read what is in literature. You could do it and I would accept. Don't laugh at me, please don't laugh at me! I didn't choose to be a deviant!'

'I'm not laughing,' said Mutumba. 'I'm dead serious. It would be against the code to use force on you even if you were not one of the Clones. It is for you to go or stay. But—you raise problems.'

Anni stared at her. 'You mean—if we had children?'

'Yes,' said Mutumba; so she was thinking of that already! 'You see, with cloning the genetic base is steady. We do not know by what chance or even not-chance He and She arrived at excellence. It was not all in the genes. Part was in experience and we have tried to copy that on all of you. I know you hate to remember the strengthening, but that's the way it has to be done. As you all understand. But if two persons of different genetic excellence were to have a child the genes would be mixed. Get back to meiosis and anything can happen.'

'It could be greater excellence,' said Anni softly.

'That is possible but not likely. There would be no genetic copying.'

'So this child would not have to get the strengthening because nobody would know what it ought to be!'

'Yes,' said Mutumba, 'I think you are correct there. Anni, did you hate the strengthening that much?'

'It's over,' said Anni quickly. Yes, thought Mutumba, they all say that. 'So, what should I do?'

'It looks to me,' said the Convener of the Council, 'that you are likely to create this new problem for us. This interesting problem. Then we shall have to hope we can come to some solution. Our job is to look at problems and try out what to do for the best. It will be of very great interest to discover how many of you there are. It's not my guess that you're the only one.' Standing up, she laid one hand on Anni's young smooth head, the plaits, the curls at the nape of the neck. Was this beauty? Or did it seem so to the Clone boy? The *toko-no-ma* in her living space held no art object, only a rather curious piece of semi-crystalline rock or metal. It was not of this earth but one of a group which the space research team had been investigating. One day when the Clones took over, it would be possible to go back to its place of origin. 'You are free,' she said, 'my child.'

'Thank you, Ma'am,' said Anni, using the formal designation, and walked softly out of Mutumba's living space and videoed Kid at Carlo's living space and saw him with the two children.

'You coming over?' he asked. 'Carlo will be at the lab quite a while. Right. I'll see you.' And Anni swam along the walkway in a secret dream where every face smiled and every light shone with bright benevolence.

Mutumba dropped her head in her hands. What was going to happen here? Above all, if the situation developed, beyond these two, power must not be used. The temptation to say no. In fact, it could be a case of protection. She began to think of a few possibilities, turning them over in her mind. Was it possible that if they, or any other Clone couple, could see the danger of meiosis, they would consider a fusing technique? In one prepared cell her nucleus could be knocked out, in another his; then the two could be fused without the uncertainties of meiosis and put back safely to nest in Anni or whatever other Clone girl might go her way. That might indeed produce a child of greater excellence.

Yes, let them have their pleasures, which normal people, like herself, could turn their minds from. It was utterly distasteful, but, as she had told Anni, not against the Code. The Council must bear this completely in mind when, as it must, the thing came to be known. She would not let it come between herself and Anni. It need not result in what was, perhaps, the sin of meiosis, if, instead, they would accept fusing. Then Anni would be both a Mum and a Clone Mum. She lifted her head, relieved. All problems have solutions.

And then she started thinking again. Was this really the solution? Was it totally acceptable? If it had come her way, would She have accepted it? This thing that had happened was something new, but she was trying to think out ways of containing it, as she knew the rest of the Council would do. Instead of going with the wave. If it was a wave. Not—not just a lapse into deviancy. If deviancy was entirely wrong, were the Clones capable of it? Or was it something which she had been looking out for, under her breath as it were, the tiny, first sign of a change. For two centuries there had been the anxiety to stabilize : when it was at last achieved that was Solution Three; the world had needed it so desperately. But now there was a counter-danger of subsiding into unquestioning confidence and security in the thought of the Clones taking over.

Hibernating dormice! This, yes, this was unworthiness. Think again. In the days of Her and Him theirs was the necessary excellence, the sudden emergence of the exact gene combination for that moment in history. But might not a slightly other kind of excellence be needed now, having to arrive through—what? A planned accident? In an unplanned plan? That Anni, back from the war, back from shock, from dead Ellen, should need something, some healing—and see and take it. And move towards solution Four?

But yet again, if deviancy was both wrong and possible for a Clone, was this like the trouble with the wheat of proved excellence? Was this the yellow spot on the rosaceae? Or was she herself too deeply conditioned into the idea of meiosis as sin?

Turning thoughts over, picking at them, discarding, considering possibilities. Quietly, her hands folded, her white-haired head a little bent, she, as Convenor, must be the one to do this turning over, and see what was wrong with the thoughts. Or right.

And there, at Miryam's living space, Kid let Anni in, but they did not touch. 'This is all new,' Kid said. 'And to me,' said Anni.

'You told her?' Anni nodded. 'That was brave.'

'She said I was free. It is not against the Code. But we are deviants.'

'Seems so. She must wonder.'

'She said it would make a problem.'

'Why?'

'Because we are Clones. We were made and born without meiosis.'

'Yes. Copies. So if we had children, and it seems we both want to do what would make that likely, they might be—

kind of jumbled. But we needn't have children. We accept the popu-policy, don't we? I can find out what deviants do. Carlo will tell me.'

Anni looked at Little Em asleep. Lu had gone back, protesting as usual. 'You'd like children, wouldn't you, Kid?'

'They might be terrific,' he said.

'Or not. We'd have to take a big chance.'

'The world would have to take it.'

'But it would be us first,' she said, and touched him lightly on the cheek with one finger and saw the glow coming under his brown skin like a fruit ripening.

CHAPTER FOURTEEN

MIRYAM was beginning to think she had some idea of what was involved in the defeat of yellow spot by the almond trees. So far she had found nothing of the kind among the affected pyruses but there was a prunus, a very thick shelled, darkish local cherry of which she had found a single specimen reviving after an infection which had apparently killed it. There were a lot of questions still to be answered. Was it or was it not coincidence that hard shells surrounding an untouched kernel had something to do with it? Now a cytologist was needed urgently. The others all said that Carlo must be flown out. She said yes in two desperate minds about it. Marvellous to see Carlo, but could they hide it? Wouldn't some touch, some look, give everything away? Could they be merely colleagues without a word or gesture to show up shockingly what else they were? Jussie of course would know and might suspect that she had sent for him on purpose.

And then—the children? Who would look after them? Would her friend who was taking care of Lu possibly have room for Little Em? She knew that her living space was already over crowded with a three year old of her own. Probably Carlo would only need to come for a few days, make his own observations and go back with specimens, but even so—well, she would have to try and video him without the others being there.

While she was worrying about this another wild wheat was found, probably not a very useful parent, but one simply didn't know. It had a slight beard and the stalk was thin; it would lodge hopelessly if grown with a fertilizer. But still their job was to get everything. 'I'd better just see the habitat, Tsing-Lo,' Miryam said, and they went off together, Tsing-Lo bouncing a little with pleasure at having made the discovery and having been praised by Miryam. Yes, Miryam thought, she's an attractive creature, these fine bones and creamy brown skin : what beyond China was in her chromosomes? She put an arm round Tsing-Lo's shoulders and at once Tsing-Lo flashed her a smile and snuggled up, extending delicate fingers round her thigh. Yes, all right, all right! But she couldn't go much further, not nearly as far as the younger woman would so clearly have liked. A pity in a way. It must be so easy to conform.

But one must also keep a close look out for anything unusual in the environment, even at ankle level, even among dry grasses and dead blackthorn tangles. Suddenly Miryam dropped to her knees and began to part the tangles. The thorns jabbed her, drawing blood; she didn't notice, though Tsing-Lo did and tried to stick on a plaster. There it was : a rubus coming alive! This particular rubus, she seemed to recall, was almost uneatable, because it had large hard seeds with only a little rather tasteless flesh round them. But of course it could, if necessary, be hybridized or mutated.

They took samples of this, as well as a cherry and almond, in the heli that whisked her and Cheng into Ulan Bator. She was feeling a certain relief at having temporarily ditched poor Tsing-Lo, who longed to come with them but had been made to feel that she would acquire much more merit by staying with Toto and getting on with field work. At Ulan Bator the Clone girls met them; they had been very worried by the fact that one of the grandees who was known to be actively hetero-sexual himself—to a revolting degree, said Jean, one of the Clone girls, dry lipped—had presided over a public whipping and branding of deviants. 'Branding?' said Cheng. 'That is new. Are you certain?'

'I saw it,' said Jean. 'It was—horrible. And he kept grinning. And everyone knew.'

'But you could succeed in understanding what it was about, what type of aggression forced them into this particular activity?'

'We did understand, at least I think so. Only I kept on also—understanding the deviants. Not the grandee. I felt only aggression towards him, or rather to the way he was living; so did many others. One was made aware of that. I think there may be a dangerous situation developing. The grandee may well be armed—illegally of course. But those others—well, they are much more within the Code.'

'It sounds as if they may have been correct to feel aggression, though it will have to be very exactly channelled. If so, no doubt you will participate,' said Miryam. Jean agreed, almost too enthusiastically. 'But you will be the first to realize that you should do nothing before time. Have you had any answer from Honan?'

'Only "message received". I think they may be away. Perhaps we should send in a full report to the Council?' asked Jean.

'Certainly,' said Miryam. 'Send a preliminary in at the same time as we send our samples.'

'We did a screen-up,' the girl said, 'but one didn't know

for certain if it was or wasn't being intercepted. But they are certainly alerted and of course we are keeping full notes. We must try to understand everyone. Including those poor, hurt deviants.'

Miryam would have liked so much to know what these young Clones' understanding of the deviants amounted to. But it would be dangerous to speak; they might understand too much. Meanwhile how to be alone when she screened up Carlo? Could that possibly be intercepted? A technical discussion. Only they'd be sure to say too much! But this was solved because Jean asked Cheng if he would come with her to a small theatre where she thought there was to be a show which would be extremely critical of the grandees. She had by now made friends whom she could trust, not least among the actors, but she did not think her language knowledge was quite enough for the fine points in the show. Cheng agreed and Miryam said yes, she would screen up her colleague and get a further line on this highly interesting development of the prunus and rubus; they had by now got the specimens, and also a report capsule from the girls ready to go off, but she had some filling in to do.

She calculated the time lag. Yes, he would be at home. But when she got through she saw something very odd indeed. Little Em was riding on the back of—not Carlo, not any of her friends. Definitely a Clone boy. She was holding on much better than she used to, but he had lifted up one arm so as to keep her safe, which meant that he was galumphing along on two knees and one hand and she seemed to be screaming with delight. Oh, Little Em! Suddenly he realized someone was screening—someone who knew the correct screen combination. He switched on from his side, shifting Little Em on to his shoulders and for one moment Miryam found herself unable to say a thing. In fact it was he who started talking. 'I'm Kid,' he said, 'Carlo is working late on the Asia material. Which you must have sent, you're Miryam, aren't you? I can tell by the way Em's shouting at you.' And indeed it wasn't too easy for either of them to hear what the other was saying and for that matter, Miryam simply didn't know what she could possibly say. It was an unimaginable situation. What could Carlo have said about them? Could this boy possibly know? But the boy smiled at her. 'Don't you be afraid one minute longer, Miryam. Carlo taught me and I'm helping him out. That's all. Look, Em, there's your mum. She's a long way off but she loves you. Do you know this, my notion is that even at this age they get right on if you talk sense to them. Now, Miryam, you screen back in an hour's time and I'll have Carlo here. Your baby's just fine now. She wasn't too good for a while, then I was able to understand her problems. Now you and she talk a bit.'

An hour later Cheng was still away and when she screened up again Carlo was there and Little Em quietly asleep. She told him about the rubus which was already on the way and about her own hunches. He gave her the cytological gen. She explained that the others had wanted him to come out but—'No,' said Carlo, 'you can do every thing that's needed on field work. Go on sending back specimens. I'd love to come as you well know but—'

'Yes, that's what I thought. Hiding. Only we mustn't let it interfere with work. However, if you really think I can do it I'll just carry on.'

'Not only that. I'm wanted here. Okay?'

'Oh—Carlo, when I screened before—'

'I know. Kid told me. It's all right.'

'But—Carlo—do you trust him?'

'How not?' said Carlo, and then: 'After all we never pretended, only conformed. He understands. I wish he could have looked after Lu as well. Lu adores him and never wants to go back.'

'Does—does Kid sleep in your living space?'

'Sometimes. If Little Em is fidgetty.'

'Carlos! You—you aren't—changing?'

'No, no, no! And we'll see one another very soon. I can't leave but they'll want you back to talk about the cereals. They'll be very happy on your triticums. They may be needed.'

'You mean something has gone wrong with the wheats? Already? Oh, that's bad.'

'It's not too certain, nor yet if it's pandemic—whatever it is. Not a virus. You'll look out?'

'The food fields here seem all right. Naturally we kept our eyes open. Where was it seen first?'

'Mexico, they say. Of all places! You've got three un-hybridized?'

'Not much use, I'm afraid.'

'Anything might be if things go badly. We just have to pack ten thousand years or so into a few seasons. Forced mutation can work very quickly. Wouldn't hurt us to be on rye bread for a while. There's more rye than we can use at the moment.'

'Barley cakes are dull. Oatcakes—well, She was brought up on them. Or so the book says. And there isn't enough anyway. Sorghum makes decent chupatties if it's milled. There was some worry over maize. How's that?'

'Nothing definite. But you never know. By the way, that rebellion was contained.'

'Which? Oh yes, I remember. Was the Council worried?'

'I hear Jussie's lover was killed.'

'That's bad luck. If anything ever happened to you, Carlo—'

'Please take care, someone may be listening. You aren't in a very healthy place.' He spoke with some urgency, for he had heard the reports about the doings at Ulan Bator and they were worrying. He doubted if even an expedition known to have been sent by the Council would be quite safe, and if anything happened to Miryam—

When Cheng came back from the theatre, amused but worried, she gave him the cytological round up and also the new threat to the wheat. They had decided on a systematic low fly over the food fields with random checks. It would be good practice for the Clone girls who had perhaps had enough of experiencing Ulan Bator.

Cheng began to tell her about the theatre audience and what had been said, implicitly and explicitly. 'The protestors are honourable people who understand the policies and want to ensure that they are viable, but not by methods which are against the code or through people who have broken the code, such as these wretched grandees. I was taken aside and told much more. It was disturbing. I have never been made aware that such inequalities could exist. Could be even tolerated! Have you?' Miryam shook her head; it had been quite unbelievable. 'This kind of thing might be the beginning of something dangerous. I would agree that the opera-plus in which we all participated on our arrival was a perfectly legitimate way of diverting aggression, but I can see the possibility of its being used to make inequalities so much worse that—well, for instance, do you realize that the grandees have other people actually working for them?'

'You mean—in their living spaces?' asked Miryam puzzled.

'Living spaces!' said Cheng. 'Whole buildings, gardens, trees! Hidden behind the ordinary blocks. I know it is difficult to believe for anyone with civilized feelings. Inside these there are workshops which make, for example, theatre costumes. The machinery is primitive, but is all owned by the grandees. Those who work there get food and only a little money—I have read about such conditions far back in early history, but never thought I would witness them. The grandees appear to have complete power. And deviancy is often found among the same type of person. It is something I find myself almost unable to speak of in front of—a colleague such as yourself.'

'I understand,' said Miryam gravely, and yes, she thought, that sort of deviant behaviour was so utterly different from Carlo and herself, but yet if Cheng knew—had she been careful enough just now screening him up? 'Cheng,' she said, 'which do you personally find more distasteful—a practiser of inequality or a deviant?'

He thought seriously: 'For me personally a deviant is more distasteful although I agree not necessarily offending against the code. But inequality and privilege are against the code and constitute direct aggression. Therefore in the widest sense persons who practise such things are the more distasteful. Do you agree, Miryam?'

But here fortunately Jean came in to say that one of the boxes of specimens for Carlo had been left behind. The computer of course insisted that the programme had been completed. Well, one couldn't expect everything to go right everywhere, especially not here.

CHAPTER FIFTEEN

THE helis were now all out. The random signal for the group was sent off and the pilot, a local woman with a long, black plait under an embroidered cap, brought it down. Miryam and Jean got out and separated; there seemed to be nothing wrong with the wheat hereabouts, great waving acres of it, almost ready for the combines. Miryam went on chance to a field of legumes, one of the improved type of lentil, but again there was nothing to worry about. Jean came to meet her with a tuft of corn. Miryam looked at it and shook her head: 'Don't worry, there's no sign of anything wrong.'

Jean said very low: 'We have instructions from the Council to monitor all long distance screenings. That included yours.' Miryam froze and waited. 'To your child. And also your—your colleague.'

'My husband,' said Miryam. 'The Council knows. We have not broken any law. Or the Code.'

Jean looked down. 'I believe you. Kid must have believed your your colleague—too. But there may be others who saw you talk. Please go on looking at the corn. She's watching.'

'It should have been private. A Council instruction to you, to monitor: yes. But who else?'

'I don't know,' said Jean, 'but I've seen people looking at you. The grandees mightn't care for you too much. They know that you may report and quicker than perhaps we can. Inequality is not only against all laws, it's against the Code. If they think that they can get you first, on deviancy —look, Miryam, I have reason to think that the pilot is in their pay and will be on the look-out and report—oh, they'll know the signs!—and then they could turn you over to the madmen and—and perhaps—Miryam, please prove you are normal.'

'With—with you?' said Miryam.

'Please. Don't you like me?'

What a question from a Clone girl! But Jean was not very old. One of the D's probably. Miryam stroked her hair and felt her shiver a little. The touch of a deviant? No fun for either of them. She wondered what to do and remembered that Tsing-Lo had not recognized her as abnormal.

She waited for a moment until the pilot was look-ing their way, then took Jean's hand and walked back with her, gazing fondly. She remembered a long time ago when she had been a schoolgirl and walked just this way with a friend. They were all being fed hormones no doubt, as well as propaganda, but some people seemed to be rather resistant, especially if their home was of a certain kind, as hers must have been, though she hadn't noticed at the time. Yes, in the end she'd been resistant. But Little Em, how would it be with her? She still couldn't get over the view of Kid. How could he? And how could Jean? Was it simply that all the Clones had this deep sense of empathy?

Close to the heli she murmured, 'Thanks. I *do* like you.' And kissed Jean on the temple below the line of the blonde hair. They took off again, both staring over the side. It would have to be repeated at the next halt.

They got back, still having seen nothing, and compared notes with Cheng. Funny, he seemed not to have sensed anything. Perhaps he was not very strongly attracted himself even in the normal way of personal relationships. Toto, who was a bit of a flirt, had clearly not been successful. Well, the popu-policy did not mean that people had got to have lovers. Cheng, she knew, was engaged in some very deep linguistic research which meant occasional very businesslike conferences with the half dozen people who were equally serious. Good luck to them if they managed to produce easier communication and better understanding. He did not have much notion of genetics but was a perfectly competent observer, as well as being their skilled interpreter, with the locals.

They went out again early the next morning, Miryam and Jean with linked arms and hands. Three halts on, near one of the new lakes, Miryam came on something which made her rather uneasy—a definite patchiness among the legumes. She took soil samples at once, also specimens of the plants. The next thing might be to question the field minders, but for this she would need Cheng. It was on her way to the heli with an armful of scrawny bean plants that Jean murmured, 'You're forgetting.' But of course! And suddenly she remembered the possible penalties—no, it was fantastic, surely. But was it? This unthinkable cruelty. She pulled Jean close; what a good, thoughtful girl she was!

But if Miryam had been normal it would be assumed that she would have a lover by now, permanent or semi-permanent. If the pilot thought about it she might consider it odd for her to be having an affair with one of the Clones.

Well, perhaps she was put down as the kind of person who behaved unfaithfully away from home! Jean had little shining curls at the back of her neck. Anyone with any sense of the fitting would put a gentle finger through them. Miryam did so. Presumably all her fellow Clones would have exactly these curls, having exactly the hair structure which produced them, but she hadn't noticed it on any of them.

On the return journey, flying high and fast and not having to look out of the heli, they sat close; the pilot could have nothing but normality to report. Indeed the only awkwardness was that Tsing-Lo was quite upset at seeing Miryam with her arm round Jean. Yet perhaps that was an additional piece of safety. Meantime the cereals seemed to be unaffected in this part of Central Asia, but there were two or three disquieting patches of abnormality among the legumes. It did not appear that these could be accounted for in any ordinary way. They talked it over hard and the Clone girls sat in, learning and understanding. Cheng promised to discuss everything with the locals, who had probably noticed that something was amiss. It was not necessarily anything serious, but the microscopic results were puzzling.

'I wonder,' said Cheng, 'if the Council will be able to tackle this adequately should it turn out to be of the nature we are assuming as a possibility.'

'They've got a good idea,' said Miryam, 'some of them, anyhow. They know it's serious.'

'So you think they are scientifically adequate?' said Cheng. 'In fact, you are defending them. You may be right, you may well be right, but I did not entirely expect it of a Professorial.'

What is he after, thought Miryam, and then no, it is

only his way of expressing himself. She looked at the others. Toto had gone back to the rack of reagents and was trying a fresh combination. Tsing-Lo was, it appeared, just sitting and looking in a puzzled way from her to Jean and back. 'I have certain doubts about the policies, but not about the code,' said Miryam tentatively. One should speak the truth when possible. Cheng nodded. 'You see,' she said, 'it's all right for us Professorials in a way. We think with our hands and eyes, work with them if you like, all this—' she waved her hand towards the microscope. 'They're only extensions. That stops us getting too silly, don't you think?' She wondered whether to go on and found that there were things she so much wanted to say—not really to Cheng but to Jean. 'Only with some people, historians, economists, the ones who don't work with their hands—well, the policies run away with them. You see, policies always have to be put into words. And nobody seems to question the policies in the really long term.'

'There is something we have found ourselves discussing,' said Jean, and Mima, the other Clone girl, who had come in, nodded and smiled her agreement.

'Well,' said Miryam, feeling very brave, 'isn't it rather like the wheat—supposing something went wrong with all of you Clones? You see it would be all if it was any.'

'You mean a physical ailment?' Jean asked.

'Not necessarily,' said Miryam. 'There could be—other things. I don't know. I don't even like to think.'

'Yet perhaps you ought to,' said Jean very seriously. 'You're a geneticist. And we ought to be told.' Cheng did not give away what, if anything, his own reaction was.

'Well, there is a danger of having too high a proportion of one kind of excellence in the population. Any population. It is even possible that another kind of excellence might be needed.' Miryam frowned, groping into herself for what she might really mean, but unable quite to come up with it. Then she went on. 'The wheat we grow almost everywhere is the best we know of. And artificially constructed. If anything happened to it, we might have to go back to something less worthy.' Now she was getting more and more embarrassed. Only the fact that the Clone girls were not, but instead were deeply interested, helped her to go on. 'We knock out more and more human genes,' she said. 'And some might have values hidden in them which we don't know.'

'This is direct criticism of the popu-policy,' said Cheng, looking straight at her. 'Do you realize this?'

'These are only thoughts,' said Miryam, suddenly rather frightened. 'And in general, as I said before, and as you know, I defend the Council!'

'You word-twisting Professorial!' said Cheng and turned to the Clones. 'That way lies deviancy!'

But Jean moved quickly. She was beside Miryam. She gave her a fond, long look. But how does she pretend so beautifully? Miryam thought, or is this because really she has turned the Clone light of understanding onto me?—and took her hand, laying her cheek on it for a moment. 'Not deviancy!' Jean said.

Tsing-Lo jumped and then looked away and went over to the bench and sat down beside Toto. 'I meant nothing personal,' said Cheng. 'It was merely an exclamation. I found that what you appeared to be leading to was—somewhat distressing.'

'I wouldn't want to distress anybody,' said Miryam. 'It may be that we are in a somewhat oppressive atmosphere. In fact, I think we should screen up our colleagues—or possibly even one of the Council members—and say we must go back. It is about time we had a general roundup. Probably all the food fields have been looked at in the same way as ours. We shall have to have detailed cytological and genetic discussions. Perhaps—' she turned to Cheng '—you would ask the people on the settlement near these legumes if they have any kind of explanation or indeed anything to say? But I doubt if they will.'

Nor had they. Cheng came back to say so and to make a rather guarded apology to Miryam. 'I had not, of course, realized that you and Jean—so few of us are fortunate enough to achieve a relationship with any of the Clone group. Will she be returning with you?'

'Unfortunately, no,' said Miryam, and found herself wishing very much that she was going to. 'But they will be reporting back on their experience within a reasonable time. In fact they are giving us a report to hand over to the Council. They are videoing back, but it would be unsafe to say too much.'

'They are very brave,' said Cheng.

'Indeed they are,' said Miryam.

CHAPTER SIXTEEN

THE Council members had heard the capsule report from Ulan Bator. Earlier there had been that short and clearly nervous video from one of the Clone girls who had been sent there for experiencing and monitoring. Could this possibly be another aggression brewing up? No more valuable lives were to be sacrificed. But there was an expedition in that part of the world doing field work on wheats. Fine, how soon could they be contacted? It was found that one at least, perhaps two, were on their way back. 'I'll make sure,' said Jussie, and videoed Carlo at his lab. His hands were stained with something or other and for that matter his lab coat and his face.

'Yes,' he said, 'she's on her way back. Toto is coming back too, but he is rather junior; he'll bring the material straight to me if you want to see Miryam. Right. She'll video the moment she touches down. No, I'm afraid we haven't come up with anything here as far as the wheats go, not yet. Disappointing. We followed up several possibilities but they didn't work out. However my colleague in Mexico has several further suggestions. But clearly there is something very interesting happening about the fruit. Naturally we'll keep the Council informed.'

Business went on while Councillors drank orange juice,

still from geniune oranges and in several flavours, since some liked straight Jaffa type and others the loose-skinned Indians or the very sweet Ghanaians, and oranges grew so prolifically that it was worth nobody's while to synthesize them. In fact, there was any amount of real fruit, all grown where it was at its best and most prolific and needed least space, but picked ripe and carried in increasingly ingenious containers. This meant that most fruits were seasonal and because of that, more enjoyable. But there were so many different kinds! People depended on having fruit all the time and in great variety; this was why the threat to the rosaceae had to be taken so seriously. Roses were taken seriously too. It might eventually stir people up to listen to newscasts and even to attend Council meetings!

Among further agenda, the Council had received a memorandum from the Clone group attached to space research who thought that there were some highly incorrect concepts among the top experts. Could they break away and start their own research, unhampered by old ideas, and if so could they have full material support? It was the first time anything like this had happened and the request must be acceded to. Not to do so would probably be against the Code, or so at least the Convenor told them. But few of the Councillors could understand the technical side and there was even a suggestion that the Clone group was rather young. Mutumba smiled briefly.

The Council adjourned for a short break, and informal talks. Shanti put a capsule into the enlarging scanner; it showed the dolphin experiments and was quite charming. The dolphins appeared to be entirely without aggression in the human sense. How restful! Perhaps one day the dolphins would decide to exercise some kind of moral pressure, at least, on their playmates. That would be fascinating; to have another species one could properly compare one's self with.

Then Miryam screened up. She was still in her expedition synthetics which looked slept in, and one finger was bandaged. They questioned her quickly about the situation at Ulan Bator. She said she thought it was boiling up and increasingly dangerous for the Clone girls. She kept on referring to Jean. They thanked her and Mutumba congratulated her on the success of her expedition. 'We'll keep in touch,' she said. Jussie added that she would feel honoured if Miryam would come over in person to her living space later that evening. It was, in fact, something of a command. Miryam would rather not have accepted, but felt she must.

It was decided not to leave this aggression to burst on its own. The means were of course available, though the Council disliked using them. It was violence and could easily become power. At two at least of the earlier moments when violence had to be used or threatened, the weapons experts had got above themselves and had to be changed. It had also led to the resignation of a very useful Council member who had found himself in danger of going against the Code. He had retreated for five years. In the end he only came back when Mutumba went off into the sub-Arctic and found him among the seals and persuaded him that he was needed. Even now he only came rarely.

Jussie screened through and after a short pause found Kid. 'Yes, she's on her way over,' said Kid. 'She was keen to get a bath and spray-on before she saw you. Don't keep her too long, will you?' he added. 'I've told Little Em she'd be back before bedtime.'

'You experts!' said Jussie. 'Keeping the rest of us on our toes.'

But if Jussie knew, thought Kid? He looked down at his own hands and turned them over, the paler palms which had stroked Anni, softly stroked all the she parts of her as she had done with his. Never, never before, had he wanted to touch a girl. He hadn't minded them. They were good friends and colleagues but there were ways one didn't want to be near them.

Was it anything to do with Carlo? With the children? With caring for Little Em so much that he found himself longing for a child of his own? It seemed impossible. Stupid. Why should it be him? He thought back, examining himself for faults as he knew he must. Everything had been straightforward until he saw Carlo all tense and worried and knew he must care. He felt some way older than his teacher whom he respected. Then suddenly Carlo spoke of his deviancy; spoke at him; spoke maybe to hurt. And he had held himself back from revulsion. From hating Carlo back. But his whole being, his social being, had tensed and quivered the same way as a soap film does almost breaking; he was shot with a whole dark spectrum of feelings, deep red and violet and black—no, he was making it up!

But he had known he must care as was laid down in the Code and he could not care unless he participated. He had supposed he could do this with the baby without involving himself with the baby's parents, but that was not the way things worked out. If he had been older and more experienced? No. And he could not speak of what he was doing to any of his group. Caring is private. It is a house against thunder and lightning. He caught himself wondering where these images he was making came from—maybe from far back, something in His childhood that had just jumped across? Something in a story His Mum had told?

Odd, so odd to be a Clone. He didn't often think this.

143

None of them did. They were proud and skilled. It was their world. And yet sometimes it seemed that there were too many of them, all alike. Not an identity crisis. They knew who they were and why; that was built in through the pain of strengthening. But being apart. Waiting to take it up—no, not power, that was a temptation, but to bring mankind, the others, into what they could be.

And now he and his fellow Clones, Chuck, Bobbi, Earl, Rod, the lot, they were not alike. No, they were not, not any longer. And the same for Anni. She had been altogether like Maggie, for instance. Now she was different. He had done that to her. And she had done it to him. And this was being deviants.

Anni. Anni. Anni. Then suddenly Little Em cried out in her sleep. He went over and settled her back and his heart turned over with love and wanting a baby daughter. Wasn't it possible that He had sometimes had such a longing? The books didn't say. Perhaps if He had He'd kept it to himself, just had to. There was so much for Him to do, He didn't have the time. And maybe He'd never met anybody He could do it with. Nobody like Anni. Or could that have been? Had He turned away because of the popu-policy and because everything was still a struggle? So were he himself and Anni wrong not to turn away? He didn't know. They all still thought of him as normal. But when they knew? Except for Mutumba: that cat knew. And she was Convenor of the Council. And perhaps she could see furthest of all. There was something Anni had said which Mutumba had told her about. A fusion technique. He had not thought properly about it while she was there. But now he must. Because this could be their child.

But meanwhile Miryam was taking on the city patterns again and how she enjoyed them! She was now washed and scented, her hair soft and wavy, and wearing a spray-on in pleasing blue greens that showed off her new walking muscles in back and legs. 'I wanted to tell you,' said Jussie, welcoming her, 'that the Council are taking immediate action at Ulan Bator. It is not public yet, but you will be anxious.'

'How immediate?' asked Miryam.

Jussie looked at the time. 'Now,' she said. 'So you need have no anxieties. The people mentioned in the report are being contacted. It will be done through them.'

'And the Clone girls, of course?'

'Naturally. Miryam, you spoke with—some warmth—about Jean. I wanted to ask you whether perhaps you are developing a relationship with her. We value you, Miryam; we value you increasingly; what you do and feel is our concern.'

For a minute or two Miryam said nothing, just looked round and then back at Jussie. She shook her head. 'I don't suppose I'm a hundred per cent,' she said. 'Who is? And I had the treatment at school. Probably it had some effect. But what I want is Carlo and the children, my own children. Sorry, Jussie, there it is. Jean. I can imagine being her lover. I hope I am her friend. You guessed right that I was very anxious about her.'

'It seems strange to me to prefer an ordinary man with all his unworthiness before a Clone girl,' said Jussie, a little sadly.

'Yes, yes, I can see that,' said Miryam. 'But I don't know that Jean would have loved me—that way. Whatever she does later on I shall watch for her and hope we meet again. And hope that she hopes the same for me. And now, Jussie,' she said abruptly, 'I am going back. Carlo will be there. We have also a great deal of scientific discussion

which we both want very much. But I am relieved to know
of the Council's decision.'

She turned and left without ceremony. And I haven't
told her about the other thing, thought Jussie. Oh well,
tomorrow. But what was the Clone boy doing in her living
space? However he was one of the lab team working with
Carlo, doing very well, and if he decided to spend his
evenings this way, that was his affair. He certainly looked
cheerful enough. But it was all a little confusing. Yes,
thought Jussie, my values seem to have become mixed.
Elissa. Already it seemed long ago. Was one always forgotten so quickly? Yes, yes, or the burden of grief would
become too much for humans to bear.

So what now? There had been so much Council work.
She hadn't managed to see how Lilac was getting on. She'd
do that now. Lilac. Yes. An interesting experiment. In the
walkway seabottom picture there was a new element;
somebody had put in the shadows of enormous predators
and the little fish fleeing; one felt one was on their scale—
perhaps on their side. Fun!

Lilac had stayed in the same living space all this time,
working, working. It was very bare; there was nothing in
the *toko-no-ma*. Nobody came near her. She cooked herself
packets of food when she felt like it, which was not often,
and slept when she was exhausted. She could have screened
up her Mum. No. Wait for Australia. Then she wouldn't
have to explain; it would be too far off. She could have
screened up Gisela. Sometimes the temptation to do this
got very strong. Poor soft golden Gisela with the light in
her hair waiting to be teased and toppled. What was she
doing now? Had she already found someone else? Did it
matter if she had? Gisela. No. No. Gisela belonged in the
gardens with the past. And she, Lilac, she had ditched

Gisela. All right, that was what she had done. Just as she had ditched her own Ninety. There were things one didn't—one couldn't—look back on. Don't turn the head. There will be a future if one can fix oneself straight ahead, and she had to master this new work. It wasn't easy. But she was going to do it. She had promised Jussie. Promises? She had made promises to Gisela. But that was in the gardens. She had blacked out the screen, shutting herself in, shutting others out.

Which meant that Jussie actually had to knock on the door, a Council member having to ask for admission! Lilac didn't even hear it at once. Then she got up and let Jussie in and there was the little bluish scar on her jawbone. They sat on the couch and talked about the work. There was a great pile of data between them including some computer statements which had clearly gone wrong somewhere. Lilac had thought she could deal with this but the programming had been a good deal more difficult than anything she had done earlier. She was rather depressed about her failure, but Jussie cheered her up, saying she was learning faster than most people. Her hand was warm and strong and lively in Jussie's, responding to praise. Elissa's hand had been like that. Then Lilac looked across the pile of papers, a deep, searching look. There was the long line of her eyes and the flicker of her brown curls. Jussie leant over and kissed her, then fell back, her eyes full of tears, but Lilac was round in a flash, kneeling beside her, looking up, young and excited and comforting. Lean back, Jussie, lean back and be comforted.

147

CHAPTER SEVENTEEN

KID and Maggie were videoing to their Clone colleague in Mexico. Here in the mega-city they were all tremendously excited. It looked as if something very important was coming up in the laboratories where the cytological examination of the prunus amygdalinus and rubus specimens from Outer Mongolia were being looked at. There was a lot of work still to be done but it seemed like a new direction for the RNA: 'We don't really know about the auxins,' Maggie said, 'we think that somehow those proplastids are involved. But when the chloroplasts are able to start developing again, membranes and all, then the whole process normalizes. We've been working with Carlo. He's so steady and he sees to it that we understand just what the problem is and how he's trying out the possible solutions. We've been in all the experimental work.'

'That's right,' said Kid. 'He's a great one to work with. Stands questions. We'll get it, Chuck. And then there'll sure be something else! How is it your end?'

'Not too good,' said Chuck. 'It's gone mighty quick. These dead fields and the dry heads scraping in the wind. The poor bastards who used to care for them all to pieces. Too true I feel sorry for them. They think to themselves it was some way their fault. We tell them no, but some

have gone back into the hills : seems they're praying. Anyway it doesn't mean they starve : not now! Could be a
bit of bread rationing on the way. Won't hurt. But we begin
to ask could it have been a big mutation in the wheat laying
it open, so to speak, to whatever is getting at it now.'

'Life and death,' said Kid, 'the great things, Chuck! And
us here to measure them.' As usual, there was one of
Maggie's plaits trailing on his arm. He gave it a little pull
and whisked it off. And Anni's were just exactly the same,
only if they'd been hers he would have tingled all over.
Remembering it, the tingling came back. What was it,
then? What had happened? He felt that if he had been
less happy, he would have been deeply afraid.

The Council were of course kept informed on the
Mexican situation, and those specially interested, such as
Jussie, were screened up after hours if there was anything;
she had done her best to cheer up Chuck, who ought not
to have been as depressed as his Professorial colleagues and
seniors, but, somehow, was. Perhaps his empathy with them
and above all the Mexican field workers was too great.
Ric had asked for immediate news of Ulan Bator. It was
so sadly clear from all that had ever gone before how useless most political interference from outside had been. It
was just possible that here there had been a sufficiently
large number of people who approved of world government, with the Council as its agent, for them to be genuinely
one with the interferers, to feel in fact that their loyalties
were not local but to the outside, to the whole of mankind.
Was this at last possible? If so it was a real forward step.
One would not know for certain at once or even for decades.
So often in the past the interferers from outside had been
on the side of the few, and these had been, normally, the
privileged, demanding protection for their higher values.

149

Would that make any difference? Outsiders were interferers, on whichever side they were. Yet this time Ulan
Bator had come up with a new answer.

People. One knows so little about them, thought Ric,
sitting in a hunch in his living space, in spite of all the
books, the social and psychological theories and experiments, in spite of all the work on the central and peripheral
nervous systems. Why do people act as they do? Why are
they so unwilling to be loved? Does love seem the same as
outside interference, is it a kind of aggression? Again and
again he wondered where Bobbi was and what he was
doing. He had taken the music poem capsule away with
him but in a rather unwilling way, or so it seemed now.
But had he ever played it? Alone?

There was an official screen-up going out to all the Councillors to say that the grandees in Ulan Bator had been dis-
armed. There was a new and relatively simple technique
for immobilizing small groups of aggressors. For the moment
they had been removed while an argument about policy
was going on, but had not yet been resolved. A really tremendous opera-plus had been put on in the great theatre
of Ulan Bator and out into the central square—singers,
acrobats, horses, camels, all mixed up with everybody. The
interferers, especially the two original Clone girls, had been
invited, indeed almost forced to attend. Meanwhile the
planes and helis were standing by.

So far so good, but the real reasons for what had gone
wrong there were still obscure. Perhaps the Clone girls
might have some idea. Was it for instance something to do
with Chinese and Mongolian history, peculiar to this
special group, or might it happen elsewhere? Ric wanted
to discuss all this, but with whom? Then came a signal,
breaking into his living space. Who was screening him up?

No, be sensible, it was not Bobbi. Would he allow entrance? Or would he just not be there?

But it was Stig speaking, asking him how things were; 'Do you need care?' Stig asked. 'I think you do. Mutumba suggested it. She has been looking at your computer's round-up on me, and her idea is that you fed in a good deal of your own trouble. If so, perhaps I can help? I might be able to understand better than others.'

'Are you feeling steady these days, Stig?'

'Well, yes. First you cared for me, and then Hiji and I came into one another's life. Strange I hadn't, so to speak, seen him. And now we think it is for ever.'

'I am glad,' said Ric. 'Hiji. Yes. He has beautiful hands. One would expect that, perhaps, with the work he is doing. But I wonder what I can have fed into that programme beyond what you told me?'

'Your interpretation, Ric. Inevitably, don't you think? It is possible that we are all having below surface doubts. And because of these doubts, because we know ourselves unworthy, we have always hoped for the takeover by the Clones. There has never been a time when we could be completely certain of ourselves without doubts, except of course in action. Afterwards the uncertainties return.'

'Yes, we were always uncertain. Except about the Code.'

'That, yes. But not necessarily even the popu-policy. Can we even be certain of that, now that it has succeeded? Does it matter any longer?'

'Flexibility. Watching for the next wave. You said that. Or did I?' Ric frowned at Stig's face on the screen. 'But surely the popu-policy, the discovery of real love—you can't mean—'

'No, no. When we saw that love must not be aggression and pain, we took the step in history. It is that step which brought me to Hiji and you to—that's why I think I might care for you. I think things have not gone well.' Stig's image in the screen looked deeply affectionate; deeply caring.

'All right,' said Ric. 'Let's meet before the Council. In the grey room : it will help me to come clear, and I need to be if I am to think positively about what is happening.'

The two Clone girls, Jean and Mima, were brought straight into the Council chamber, rather embarrassed at still wearing the clothes they had fought and flown in, but pleased to see Anni who had been asked to sit in. There might be similarities between the two situations that had flared up and been dealt with. And then Anni's comments would be useful. Jussie looked with special interest at Jean : if she had been in Miryam's place she would have loved Jean and been terribly anxious about her. As she had been about Elissa. But Jean had come back.

Provisionally all was well; that was the report. The equitable distribution of living space in Ulan Bator was now taking place. It was urgent that erring wives of grandees and the surplus population they had produced, sometimes not willingly, should be protected and treated within the Code. But all kinds of jubilation were in order and could be encouraged. Two of the grandees had been killed, battered to death by the rest of the population. 'Could you have protected them, Jean?' Mutumba asked.

'I could have tried,' said Jean, 'but they had not behaved in a fully human way. I told you. It helped the others, killing them. After it, they could come fully within the Code. The grandees were only part of a thing.' She was not at all worried. 'I see,' said Mutumba. And Ric, taking it in, remembered an episode in His life, sometimes perhaps glossed over, when something of the same kind had happened. But a few of the Council looked uneasy. Yet, this was a Clone, one of the future speaking.

Jussie had been with Mutumba before the meeting, having what had started with discussion on the wheat situation : what earlier data existed of a major mutation in cereals? Could it be accounted for in any way? 'It doesn't seem entirely certain that it is all due to a mutation,' said Jussie, 'they are still working on several lines, most of which will be negative no doubt. The latest news in the field is a spread to North America and possibly Europe, though some can probably be harvested there. That doesn't look like a mutation, but then we still have very little idea of how natural mutations are caused. This is very long-term research, and most of the first ideas that came up, turned out to be unsound. However, it's as well we have a gene pool of triticums, even if it doesn't look like a very good one, in case there's major reconstruction needed.'

'A wheat pool,' said Mutumba. 'Okay. But are we sure, Jussie, are we quite sure, that we shall never need to get ourselves a human gene pool? And as varied as it comes? Now, Jussie, I'm asking you to think in these terms : a kind of excellence which exactly fitted a certain epoch might, soon or late, need certain alterations. The wheat was the best of its species : something went wrong. Now we have to start again. With more knowledge. Using the good wheat, sure, but back crossing to something we thought we'd finished with. Yes?'

'Mutumba, you are not saying you have doubts about—about the Clones? You can't!' Jussie felt as though there had been an explosion deep down, the far end of the mine—at the face—in the dark—

'Not exactly. No. At present I have no doubts. They have done extremely well. Yes, as well as we hoped. Any

153

of us. But isn't it possible they may have doubts about themselves? Or other feelings.'

'You mean—what?' Jussie stared at her, trying to read behind her eyes.

'I am not certain, Jussie. I'm feeling my way. Suppose they were lonely. Felt cut off. I've got to see a way for them—and us.'

'Towards what, Mutumba?' The Convenor's fingers seemed to be trying to hold onto something that slipped.

'That's it. If I knew. If I was certain. Just certain. Could be towards Solution Four. I don't know yet. But it could be that we can't afford to let too many human genes slip out. In case there was need some time. Unworthy. Of course we are. But the need might come. Did you ever think what other genes there could have been in Him and Her? The ones that didn't combine? Don't you be upset, Jussie. I ask you now to think.'

Jussie was upset, yes. One can't just think in an ordinary way about something which has been a certainty, a sacred certainty, from the very start of one's thinking life. What she told the Clone Mums. Deep in her like the music of a song which told everything. Why must Mutumba—but she pulled herself together. 'They used to talk about genetic engineering,' she said, 'the kind that is done with plants. And some animals. Insects. But humans—no. Nobody speaks that way.'

'Genetic engineering was against the Code. Clearly. Don't you remember what She said about it at the Dunedin conference? Not much, but—concise. No, we don't want that.'

'Then tell me what it is you see, Mutumba.'

'If I ever see clear I'll tell you. Could be it will not be me that sees, but them. The Clones themselves. All the same I am getting sure that there must somehow be a gene pool ready. In case.'

'But from where? Mutumba, you don't mean——'

'Maybe I do. Maybe I don't. There's plenty to be weighed up. You can get to a place by a hundred roads. This is between you and me, Jussie, for now.'

'But we can't just reverse a policy without landing the world in guilt and misery!'

'That's not the way it should be done,' said Mutumba. 'Nor will it. None of us need be guilty. We have done right. But also we can change that right. Gently.' She stood up tall, folded in purple, her feet beautiful still in the lightest of sandals firmly treading the soft carpeting. And suddenly Jussie thought, but of course, we could get Clones from her!

And now this thought kept on coming back to Jussie. It was not necessary to have Clones from the completely excellent, from Him and Her, but from those who had proved themselves by their whole lives to be devoted and other-regarding, acting always within the Code, people from whom a child could be proud to be a Clone. Who else in the Council? Andrei? She didn't know. If Elissa—stop! But of course that mightn't have been in Mutumba's mind at all. She might have been thinking of allowing the hetero-sexuals to go on in the place which the popu-policy had genuinely not reached. Not all deviants, of course. But perhaps some of the most skilled and other-regarding Pro-fessorials. People like Miryam and Carlo.

Ric and Stig came in together. It had been a good meet-ing in the grey room, that curious place where the water which flowed through the Council chamber came bubbling up, actually from one of the borings which supported the supplies for the mega-city: fossil water from a great depth, fantastically cold. It came into a black basin and flowers were planted all round, small green and white orchids, creeping rushes and suchlike. The lights came softly from under the water or on the sides of the streamlet as it was warmed to surface temperature after who knew how long so far below. Ric had found himself able to speak with Stig and at the same time the shape of a music poem began to come into his mind, a poem of farewell and resignation but also, in some way and strangely, about something else of whose nature he was still unaware, of hope.

Jussie did not stay till the end of the meeting. Andrei wanted to discuss his Aral Sea plan, to get Council approval, and then to leave as soon as possible, with powers. This he would certainly get. There was also the food problem, but here a master plan of alternatives had long been in existence, though clearly it would need updating. It would depend on whether other cereals were affected. So far there was no trouble about maize, though naturally a maize-based diet would have to be fortified. Oats seemed safe, and up to the present rice, and probably rye. But there would have to be a quick stepping up of areas cultivated with alternatives and tests on the land from the dead crops. That was already in hand. The technical discussion and action would now be continuous but at least there could never again be the horror of some groups making a profit out of other people's hunger and death.

One other thing had happened. There were a few spectators in the gallery, listening in, something which had not happened for a long time. Interest. Participation. Council members looked up, pleased, with a nice feeling that they were being noticed again. Soon perhaps, there would even be questions.

But Jussie wanted to see Miryam again. She screened her up and asked her to come over to the main gate of the

western rose garden, not too far from her lab. It was one of
the largest and most beautiful of the rose gardens with ter-
races and mounds and sizable trees where the climbers
ramped. People who were interested in new roses came there
a great deal to see the new varieties and argue about their
merits, occasionally going so far as to pull one up by the
roots. The rose season had been prolonged from May to
November, but even in the deepest resting period of winter
it was beautiful, as there was clever alternative planting,
drifts of cyclamen and crocus bulbs and low foliage plants
between the rose bushes and here and there statues and
fountains. No doubt it would have been possible to breed
all the year roses, but that would have destroyed the
seasonal joy. Around the garden were some of the earlier
Scandinavian-built blocks of living spaces.

Miryam was a little cross. Why was Jussie interrupting
her again? Yet she was glad to see the roses, so many
types! If only one could be sure they would be all right.
However rose pips were extremely hard; that was something
to make one hopeful. It was what Jussie started on: 'Are
you going to be able to save the roses, Miryam?' she asked.

'It's not certain yet,' said Miryam, 'but we think we're
on the track. My colleague believes he has found the seat
of the viral infection and what, so far, appears to check it.
That's the first step.'

'It would be a pity for you if we lost the roses,' Jussie
said, 'because some of these living spaces have been re-
distributed and one has been allocated to you.' She pointed
up towards one of the blocks. It had a green copper roof
and balconies facing into the sun.

'Here?' said Miryam. '*Here*? Are you sure?'

'We'll go up,' said Jussie, and noticed that Miryam had
gone quite white.

157

The correct door touch opened into the empty living space. Miryam took one look and ran across, yes, it was a balcony looking over the rose garden! Clearly one could have it open, breathe real air, and there was a plant box in the corner—for the children! If that didn't upset her neighbours. But Jussie must have thought—plant boxes had stayed in all the old Scandinavian blocks; some people found them dirty or uncouth and didn't know what to do with them. Not Miryam! She came back and looked again. The living space wasn't quite as big as her old one, only there was an archway with little shelves in the side. She went through. 'But there are *two* rooms,' she said, 'Jussie—surely not for me? Wouldn't that be privilege—luxury—against the Code?'

'You've done well,' Jussie said, 'and someone has to have these rather old-fashioned living spaces. The screen doesn't expand, I'm afraid, not like the new ones—'

However Miryam paid no attention, she was still exploring. 'But there's all this room for the instant ray—and—oh, I could do cooking! I've always longed to do cooking, it must be such fun!'

'You may find you have to put in a new disposal unit,' said Jussie, 'and perhaps a mixer for the shower—'

'Look, if I put my desk here and—yes, there's the music outlet—and my books—oh Jussie, two rooms! You don't know what it means. The children—'

'And apparently Kid.'

'He's been such a help to Carlo. And to me. Ever since I came back. Dear Kid. I never thought I could find myself so—so humanly fond of a Clone boy. He—he takes trouble to make people happy: I think his empathy must be very well expanded and controlled. He stopped me feeling bad about the children.'

'Really!' said Jussie. 'In view of the popu-policy with which you agree in general, was this correct?'

'Yes!' said Miryam. 'My children may be as valuable as you say Carlo and I have been. We'll try to make them valuable, Jussie, not just surplus population. Kid will help with that; they love him. Oh Jussie, looking out—I feel quite giddy! I could grow flowers myself!'

'They won't be as good as the flowers down in the garden. Or even art-flowers,' said Jussie, but her voice wasn't unkind. 'And this kind of air is really no better, in fact temperature control is very difficult. And if you open the balcony glass, things will blow in. Dust. Leaves.'

'Leaves,' said Miryam to herself, 'real leaves.' And sure enough she opened every bit of balcony glass—these out of date Scandinavian catches!—and leant over, looking three storeys down into the rose garden, but only just above the tallest trees. There was a perceptible south breeze and in the mega-cities there were none of the city smells which had, so the books said, formed such an unpleasant background in the late twentieth century. She was examining the tall trees first, taking in the leaf shape, the rustle, the slight turn from upper to lower leaf colour as the wind stirred them. In leafless winter one would see down to the winter bulb drifts. She murmured tree names: 'Linden. Plane. Walnut. Hornbeam. Rowan. Aspen. Lovely names, aren't they!'

'Un-scientific,' said Jussie sternly, but gave it away with a small giggle.

But Miryam was still looking along the shelter line. 'Ailanthus. There's an evergreen—oh, a Kashmir cypress! Two oak species. Oh Jussie, Jussie. There's the New Zealand notofagus.' But the roses themselves! She was now looking beyond to the green hillocks where species roses grew;

backed by suitable small trees and bushes. 'That clump of
lilacs with the weeping beech behind—no, Jussie, *there*!—
it's over now, but next Spring, oh I shall see them and smell
them!'

Next Spring, thought Jussie, and where will my Lilac
be? But Australia isn't so far. And she is now entirely not
afraid. 'Over behind that tree—whatever it is!—is the
experimental area. See, Miryam? Where there's a group
working.' She pointed.

But Miryam was leaning further over the copper balcony.
'Just underneath—I wonder which birch that is, there are
so many. You know, we may have to replant all the prunus
and pyrus. But if the rapid growth hormones are used they'll
catch up in a few seasons. Oh, magnolia sargentiana! And
look, Jussie, those acers have red and golden leaves that
blow in Autumn. I have a poem that a Japanese colleague
wrote. They circle in the wind. Jussie, will the new, smaller
cities that are being planned all have gardens like this?'

'That's an idea, Miryam. So that people can meet in a
thoroughly good environment. Perhaps you'll be able to
help. They'll all need rosaceae.'

'Such places for children . . . Oh Jussie, I'm sorry!'

'That's all right, Miryam. It's not impossible that there
might be some planned alterations of policy.'

'Do you mean—I could take Lu and Em into—this
garden? Without upsetting people?'

'Just be careful, Miryam. At first. But—anyhow those
leaves will blow in! And no doubt you'll be on the garden
committee!'

'What fun, what fun . . .'

'So you're happy,' said Jussie, and then, 'There are so
many kinds of happiness. According to the genes.'

AFTERWORD

Naomi Mitchison:
The Feminist Art of Making Things Difficult

I first discovered Naomi Mitchison's *Solution Three* in the National Library of Scotland. What I found there was no bound book, however, but its earlier version: two cardboard, wide-lined spiral notebooks containing the longhand draft of a novel entitled "The Clone Mums." The title intrigued me immediately. I had come to Great Britain to investigate the literary representation of the new reproductive technologies, and had spent months reading novels ranging from Margaret Atwood's *The Handmaid's Tale* to Fay Weldon's *The Cloning of Joanna May,* and following the parliamentary debates about human embryo research in the British press and *Hansard,* the parliamentary record.[1] I had seen how contemporary works of fiction joined journalism and public documents to portray the social disruptions of embryo experimentation, in vitro fertilization, surrogate motherhood, and fantasies of cloning human embryos. But I was unsettled by what I found in Scotland: a manuscript imagining the impact of these reproductive technologies written when they were still only hypothetical. According to the scrawled date on the inside cover of the first spiral notebook, Naomi Mitchison wrote "The Clone Mums" in November 1970, eight years before the inaugural moment of that new medical field: the 1978 birth of the first test-tube baby, Louise Brown.

Even before I began to read, the spiral notebooks held tantalizing clues to the manuscript inside. On the inside front cover, I found the scrawled and cancelled draft of a dedication: "To Jim Watson who (so to speak impregnated me with the idea of this book) first suggested this horrid idea, & Anne MacLaren [sic] who encouraged it & made it manageable."[2] This ambivalently phrased homage to James Watson, co-discoverer with Francis Crick of the double helical structure of the DNA molecule, and to Anne McLaren, a leading British embryologist—two scientists deeply immersed in research foundational to modern genetic medicine and in vitro fertilization—announced Naomi Mitchison's complex personal engagement with contemporary science.[3]

Spurred on by this initial discovery, I went on to read the notebooks themselves, with excitement if often with difficulty due to Mitchison's minute scrawl. I found there a novel with a wonderfully diverse cast of characters—lesbian, gay, and straight, of many races and cultures, from all parts of the (future) world—all trying in different ways to build an emancipatory society based upon a new model for reproduction and childrearing. I found a novel that lived up to its provocative dedication to James Watson, in its exploration of the specifically feminist challenge posed by Watson's new genetics, and to Anne McLaren, in its vision of reproductive control based on projected developments in embryology and reproductive technology. Finally, I found a novel that explored the feminist temptation to use reproductive technology to eradicate sexism, racism, and war, and to produce instead a peaceable, uniform, and predictable society.

Although written in 1970, Mitchison's novel contains a remarkable critique of reproductive technologies that would not come into wide use until the 1990s. But the medical interventions into human reproduction that *Solution Three* addresses have a history spanning the entire twentieth century, beginning with the program of reproductive incentives and disincentives advocated by the early twentieth-century eugenics movement and extending through what we now know as artificial insemination, in vitro fertilization, surrogate motherhood, post-menopausal embryo implantation, and (the most recent technique to achieve at least laboratory success) the cloning of human embryos.[4]

Fascinated by this novel that so bravely staked out a field that was, in 1970, little more than a scientist's fantasy, I tried to find out whether it had ever been published. After searching libraries in

Scotland and England, I finally discovered its published version under a different title: *Solution Three*. Why the title change? Early twentieth-century eugenics had come to a frightened halt with the revelations of the Nazi Final Solution, as its racial purity campaign led to horrors of human experimentation and to death camps. Mitchison's title change invokes this history, with all its individual and social terrors, but with a crucial twist.

Changing the title from "The Clone Mums" to *Solution Three,* Mitchison broadened the novel's scope, implicitly urging us to attend not only to the impact of reproductive technology on individuals (the women who served as surrogate mothers and the children conceived by cloning) but also to its impact on society at large. By conceiving of a "Solution Three" that follows the Final Solution, Mitchison probed the implications of using reproductive control strategies not to produce a master race, but rather to create a society in which racism, sexism, and militarism are no more.

What gave Naomi Mitchison the remarkable ability not only to predict the new science of reproductive technology, but to anticipate some of its most troubling social implications? Coming from a family of scientists and living in a culture that increasingly reveres scientific practices, where did she find the courage of her feminist convictions, the courage to tackle the social dangers of science head-on? Although such creative bravery will always ultimately be mysterious, we can glean some answers from Mitchison's life as well as from her other writings.

Born in Edinburgh in 1897 into a world of intellectual and social privilege, Naomi Haldane spent her childhood in Oxford, where her father was a Reader at New College, and at Cloan—the Haldane family estate in Perth, Scotland.[5] She was educated at Lynam's School and St. Anne's College, Oxford, and after a stint as a volunteer nurse during the First World War, she married G.R. (Dick) Mitchison (later Lord Mitchison) in 1916, and raised a large family—three sons and two daughters. She describes herself as coming "from a family of scientists": her grandfather was John Burdon Sanderson; Regius Professor of

Physiology at Oxford; her father was the celebrated physiologist John Scott Haldane; and her beloved older brother, J.B.S. Haldane, would grow up to be a well-known physiologist, geneticist, and popular science writer, one of the "visible college" of Cambridge socialist scientists who crucially shaped British science policies.[6] Among her close childhood friends, so nearly kin that no chaperones were ever required when young Naomi spent time with them, were Julian Huxley, who would later make his mark on scientific thinking as an eminent zoologist and prominent popular science writer, and his younger brother Aldous, author of a classic modern portrait of the scientific control of reproduction, *Brave New World*.[7]

Along with that male world of intellectual accomplishment, Naomi was also exposed to a powerful tradition of independent thinking through the women of her family and circle of friends. A Conservative backer of Empire despite her husband's Liberal politics, Naomi's shingle-haired mother, Louisa Trotter Haldane, was a staunch suffragist who "always supported women in the professions, went to a woman doctor when possible, and encouraged [Naomi] to think of medicine as a career."[8] Her Aunt Bay (Elizabeth Haldane) was a writer and the first Scottish woman to be named a Justice of the Peace; her grandmother was a Victorian matriarch who held court from her extensive estate at Cloan, in the north of Scotland, enjoining on the family a life of self-sacrifice and distinction. Close family friends included "Aunt" Florence Buchanan, the distinguished, if somewhat difficult, physiologist whom Naomi's mother championed as a feminist, and Marie Stopes, the paleobotanist, whose far more celebrated activities as a birth control educator were politely ignored.[9]

As Jill Benton's perceptive biography reveals, Mitchison's life included the same intense political and social involvement that characterized the lives of many of her family and friends, but with a difference.[10] A lifelong social reformer, birth control educator, and passionate partisan of Scottish nationalism, Mitchison's commitments have extended beyond Scotland and England to Africa. Not only did she run as Labour candidate for Parliament in 1935, serve as a member of the Argyll County

Council from 1945 to 1966, and as a member of the Highland Panel (1947–1964) and the Highlands Development Council (1966–1976), but she also served as the tribal adviser and "Mmarona" (mother) to the Bakgatla of Botswana from 1963 to 1969.[11] The result of a friendship with Linchwe, next in line to be chief of the Bakgatla, whom she met at one of the many parties she gave at her home in the Scottish Highlands, Carradale House, during the 1950s and 1960s, this last political office is less a departure from Mitchison's Scottish nationalism than a continuation of her interest in social justice. Benton explains that the position appealed to Mitchison because "the Bakgatla had a chance ... to exploit science and technology. . . . She hoped to help her tribe rework the mechanisms of history and to avoid the pitfalls of individualism and capitalism."[12]

The feminist, scientific, and social sympathies produced by these early influences also leave their mark on the wide-ranging adult writings of Naomi Mitchison. She gave us not only the prophetic critique of reproductive technology that is *Solution Three,* but also her classic meditation on feminist science, *Memoirs of a Spacewoman* (1962), and the challenging portrait of Western genetic engineering and agribusiness, *Not by Bread Alone* (1983).[13] And there are nearly a hundred other works, too: from plays, historical novels, and fairy stories to African tales, social commentary, and popular science works for adults and children. Mitchison's rightful fame for her science fiction is still ahead of her, for feminist interest in that genre has grown dramatically in recent years. Her most celebrated works to date have been *Memoirs of a Spacewoman* and her historical novels: *The Conquered* (1923), *Cloud Cuckoo Land* (1925) and *The Corn King and the Spring Queen* (1931).[14] Set in the Roman Empire, in fifth-century Greece, and in Egypt, Greece, and Sparta of the third century B.C. respectively, these novels use unfamiliar contexts to articulate critiques of contemporary gender relations, giving prominence to the lives and concerns of women.

By the time *The Corn King and the Spring Queen* was published, Mitchison had found celebrity. Winifred Holtby ranked that novel as the very first when she compiled a list for *The Bookman* of the six most significant novels published in 1931. Yet if in Holtby's opinion Mitchison's novel outstripped even Virginia Woolf's *The Waves,* most other reviewers still seemed mystified by its feminist vision. "Reviewers, mainly men, saw only the masculine elements of the novel and were blind to [the heroine's] quest for psychological wholeness and historical adventuring."[15] A later novel, *We Have Been Warned* (1935), met not just critical incomprehension but actual censorship when she submitted it to her publisher, Jonathan Cape.[16] Cape had been fined for publishing Radclyffe Hall's *The Well of Loneliness* (a cause which Mitchison had joined other writers in supporting), and was still struggling with the adverse publicity that the trial had brought his press. The frank portrayal of female sexuality and contraceptive use in *We Have Been Warned* reopened all the anxieties raised by the Radclyffe Hall case, and Cape asked Mitchison to rewrite explicit passages. She angrily refused, and after twelve years with Jonathan Cape, she took her novel elsewhere. The book then went the rounds of publishers, was refused by both Victor Gollancz and John Lane, and was published at last by Constable.[17]

All of Mitchison's writings reflect the dual commitment to social activism and feminist imagination that made *We Have Been Warned* so troubling to a publishing world still rocked by the *Well of Loneliness* trial. But one work in particular illuminates the original feminist vision contained in the two deceptively drab cardboard-bound spiral notebooks I discovered with such excitement in the National Library of Scotland: "Saunes Bairos: A Study in Recurrence."

"Saunes Bairos": Preview of Mitchison's Feminist Critique

We can trace the iconoclastic feminist perspective, the sympathies for the outsider, and the interest in the social implications of scientific practice characteristic of Mitchison's adult works back to a play she wrote when only fifteen years old: "Saunes Bairos: A Study in Recurrence." Although not her first play, this was the first to achieve a fully staged production. It opened on May 5th and 6th, 1913, at the Oxford Preparatory School, Oxford, England, under the direction of Lewis Gielgud. The cast for the premiere performance included her close friends Aldous and Trevenen Huxley, Dick Mitchison, who would later become her husband, and her brother J.B.S. Haldane. Naomi herself took the starring role.

Though the players were all secondary school-aged children, the topic, like most of the audience, was definitely adult. To an audience comprised of a cross section of the British scientific and professional elite, who would later form an important part of the mainstream and reform eugenics movements in early twentieth-century Britain, the play dramatized the global implications of the scientific control of reproduction. Since the founding in 1907 of the Eugenics Education Society, the eugenic program for controlling human reproduction in order to improve the human species had been gaining increasing numbers of proponents, who were attracted by its implicit promise of human perfectibility. Against a background of British concern about hereditary physical and psychiatric diseases, the eugenics movement advocated a combination of positive incentives for the reproduction of those judged physiologically and psychologically healthy with regulations and programs designed to discourage reproduction among the "unfit."[18] "Saunes Bairos: A Study in Recurrence" anticipates *Solution Three* in its critique of the political uses of such eugenic programs of reproductive control.

Set in the year 1200 in a nation high in the Andes, the play recounts the attempt by a small band of resisters to escape a society that has turned reproductive control to oppressive ends. The ruling High Priests of the nation of Saunes Bairos have instituted a reproductive regime known as the "Law," which controls the number of births and the sex of the children born and forbids travel beyond national boundaries. Using this Law, the High Priests plan to breed a "perfect race," and so conquer the world.

Mitchison's protagonists, the sister and brother Carila and Coraxi, plan to outsmart the High Priests and escape their restrictive society. Yet only Carila can bring their plans to fruition, because her skeptical relation to authority and tolerance for difference gives her the independence and flexibility necessary to learn the priestly password required to venture down the mountain to lands below the snowline. In contrast, her brother Coraxi refuses to question the authority of the priestly fathers, and he finds himself trapped in Saunes Bairos, subject to the rule of a new, but equally oppressive, regime.

If in its sibling protagonists Naomi's play has an autobiographical tinge, it also has a critical and feminist perspective on Western science unusual in one born and bred so close to the seat of patriarchal power. As its subtitle suggests, "Saunes Bairos: A Study in Recurrence" argues that an eugenic program of reproductive control would be the destruction of any nation, whether thirteenth-century Saunes Bairos or twentieth-century England. Like Katharine Burdekin's *Swastika Night* (1937), "Saunes Bairos" articulates the processes by which reproductive control can become a kind of religion, enforced on women's bodies by patriarchal quasi-priests who use it to further both racist and sexist ends.[19]

Given its eugenic and genetic themes, "Saunes Bairos" was guaranteed to interest a large proportion of its Oxford audience, and press clippings reveal that there was enthusiastic applause at the premiere.[20] Yet the reception was not wholly enthusiastic. Naomi's play also met with some criticism, from those members of the audience who considered it inappropriate for her, a young girl of fifteen, to address a topic so closely linked to sexual matters. Indeed, following the premiere performance, her mother received several letters protesting the play's unsuitable topic. Mrs. Helen Cooke, whose daughter Mary was also in the cast, sent a letter edged in black protesting:

> The introduction of eugenics into the play, by such an apostle & in so crude & public a way is what distresses us so much. That the study of this subject is needed is very evident to any thoughtful and observant being, but it is one that requires careful & wise handling, and to be taught at other times than during a play, written by a clever but necessarily very inexperienced child of 15.... Naomi says girls are brought up in too great ignorance of this subject—Are they? And is her narrow experience of girls and her condemnation of their Mothers' [sic] ideals and their methods excuse enough for her to take the matter out of their hands and without warning speak as she did and make others speak? I am

ambitious for Mary and her sisters, but I prefer to aim at something more for her, than to be chosen by her mate for good breeding qualities. I still believe in Men's [sic] reverence for women. Had the teaching been given by you or Mr. Haldane, with an announcement of its intention, it would have been welcomed by most people. But by Naomi—NO![21]

Such critical letters in response to "Saunes Bairos" reflect the pervasive gender role expectations that governed Naomi's upbringing, as well as the sexual double standard that shaped her education. While scientific curiosity in boys was applauded, and Naomi remembered her father addressing his young son, Jack, as a fellow scientist, the same impulse in girls was more problematic, as Mitchison recalled:

I grew out of childhood into a healthy respect for scientific curiosity and work, but I never had my brother's early understanding of it, and I wonder, now, whether this was temperamental or whether certain avenues of understanding were closed to me by what was considered suitable or unsuitable for a little girl. Not deliberately closed, I think, since both my parents believed in feminine emancipation, but—there is a difference between theory and practice.[22]

Little wonder that she remembered herself having a "love-hate relation with science" and ultimately decided—as she recalls in her autobiography—"I had to give up scientific practice and, instead, write."[23]

Yet if Naomi abandoned scientific practice, the theme of science continued to fascinate her throughout her life, having been ingrained in her from childhood. Like her older brother, she was exposed early to her father John Scott Haldane's scientific investigations, for his physiology laboratory adjoined their Oxford home, Cherwell. Indeed, she made an early appearance in his papers, as a subject of scientific inquiry: "N.H., six years old, four feet high, weighing 25.2 kilos, and with rather well-developed lung area."[24] Later, her favorite occupation—shared with her brother—was not tennis or croquet, but guinea pig breeding. She felt deep empathy for the guinea pigs she studied: "I certainly anthropomorphised too much, but I don't suppose anyone else has ever watched guinea pigs in this way; scientifically they are an exploited race."[25]

As feminist critics of science have documented, since the scientific revolution of the seventeenth century nature has been portrayed as the feminized subject of male scientific knowledge.[26] Seen as closer to nature than men are, women have historically been in complex relation to the scientific project, understood as both object and subject of scientific inquiry. Naomi's empathy for the guinea pigs reflects this intertwined understanding of nature and woman. It attests to her own sense of marginality: positioned between the experiences of human beings and of animals, and between the subject and the object of science. The feeling not only recalls Naomi's early experiences as her father's experimental object of study, but it also suggests a powerful inspiration for her writing about science. This empathy for one "exploited race"—guinea pigs—may have led to her dramatic portrait of another: the South American peoples of the nation of Saunes Bairos.

More than half a century later, in *Solution Three,* Mitchison returned to the theme that informed "Saunes Bairos": the use of people as experimental subjects, or human guinea pigs, and the scientific project of achieving reproductive control. While in her adolescent drama Naomi Haldane attacked a society that used reproductive science to further oppressive, patriarchal, and ethnocentric ends, sixty years later she would wonder whether the outcome would be better if reproductive technologies were deployed towards feminist, emancipatory ends. Even though the Nazis had used eugenics to enforce their own horrific aim of racial superiority, could a progressive state use eugenic methods to do away not only with racial prejudice, but with the very concept of race itself? Could such methods also eradicate homophobia, sexism, and excessive aggression? These questions set the daring premise for Mitchison's *Solution Three.*

The premise is daring because it addresses an idea long repressed within feminism: that there is an appeal (even to feminists) in the idea of a "technological fix" to social problems. In 1972, Shulamith Firestone suggested in *The Dialectic of Sex* that the problems of our oppressive society might be cured not by social technologies but by medical science: the "more distant solutions based upon the potentials of modern embryology, that is, artificial reproduction, possibilities still so frightening that they are seldom discussed seriously."[27] Firestone was right: such possibilities are frightening, as demonstrated by the speed with which Firestone's tract was dismissed by feminist theorists. Rather than exploring technologically produced alternatives to childbearing, feminist psychoanalytic social critics of the 1970s focused their attention on different options for child rearing. Two of the most widely read and influential studies, Dorothy Dinnerstein's *The Mermaid and the Minotaur* (1977) and Nancy Chodorow's *The Reproduction of Mothering* (1978), explored the roots of violence and sexual oppression in the practice of woman-only mothering (or, to put it another way, male un-involvement with child rearing). They advocated not new technologies to liberate women from the burden of pregnancy, but new social technologies—shared childcare practices—to liberate all people from the "human malaise" produced by what Dinnerstein delineated as "the female monopoly of early child care."[28] Nearly alone in her anticipation of Firestone, Mitchison took up the notion of a "technological fix." In *Solution Three*, she investigated the social implications of using reproductive technology to cure social problems and demonstrated that even the most well-intentioned projects for reproductive control have unexpected costs.

While Firestone advocated instituting universal extra-uterine gestation to abolish the pain and social burden of pregnancy, *Solution Three* takes a broader approach. Rebuilding from a devastating nuclear war, the Council of Mitchison's future state turns to reproductive technology to solve a problem of human aggression, caused by a rising population and a drastically falling rate of food production, which had nearly resulted in species suicide. After a cycle of war, overpopulation, food shortage, famine, and resulting violence, the Council adopts a policy known as "the Code." This reproductive regime consists of three sweeping edicts: heterosexuality is forbidden, homosexuality is mandated, and reproduction occurs primarily by cloning, from the black American man and the white woman from the Shetland Islands (referred to simply as "He" and "She") who are the world's heroes. Their clone progeny are gestated by state-chosen surrogate mothers, called "Clone Mums," whose reproductive destiny is an honor and a privilege. Once born, the clone children are raised in collective childcare centers until, at roughly the time of weaning, they show signs of creative and individualistic play. Then they are taken from their gestational mothers and subjected to a process known as "the strengthening," through which their individuality is effaced, to be replaced by a set of conditioned responses.

The goal of the reproductive technology central to "the Code" is to replace dangerous difference with safe sameness. Mitchison signals in her foreword that we must attend to the biological meaning of difference. She takes the unusual step of providing her readers with definitions of two biological terms, clone and meiosis:

1. A clone consists of the descendants of an individual produced through a-sexual reproduction, having identical genetic constitution.

2. Meiosis is a cell division in the germ cell line during the formation of eggs and sperm, which results in the chromosome number being halved and the genes re-assorted. Note that, when egg and sperm cells re-unite in the process of fertilization, one chromosome in a pair comes from each parent, so that the original number of chromosomes comes back, but there may be crossing over of chromosome material. (6)

To a contemporary reader, Mitchison's reproductive plot surprises not just in its prescient scientific focus, but in its anticipation of contemporary feminist issues. Cloning and meiosis can be understood not only as biological events, but as metaphors. Seen thus, they invoke one of the hottest recent feminist debates: the issue of identity and difference. By adopting "Solution Three" and shifting from meiosis to cloning, Mitchison's future world is attempting to eradicate aggression, sexism, heterosexism, and racism all at once. In short, it is attempting to wipe out difference—not only on the biological level, but on the social as well.

If the brutal oppressions of Nazi eugenics characterized the "Final Solution," Solution Three relies instead on the softer coercions of a gentle eugenics: those who are unwilling to abide by the mandated homosexuality, or who wish to reproduce in vivo, are given substandard housing and less job access and are subjected to the chilly climate that we know, from our own time, can so hamper the performance of women and people of color in the workplace. The goal of this new, softer eugenics, and this new method of reproduction, is to narrow the population pool down to a nearly stable number, in which clones predominate. These identical copies—both physical and psychological—of the activist leaders who founded the state are designed to be nonviolent and non-sexist. Rendering marginal those unstable heterosexuals who contribute to violence and social unrest, and producing a solid center of genetically and psychologically uniform individuals, Mitchison's new state hopes to avoid the instability that had almost proven humanity's downfall.

As a simple glance at the science section of the daily papers will reveal, those who rely on "Big Science" to solve social problems are not always vindicated. Nor is the pursuit of ideologically correct uniformity always a viable social goal, as feminist debate has so powerfully demonstrated in the last ten years.[29] Mitchison's narrative illuminates with ironic accuracy the flaws in such plans. *Solution Three* opens with the discovery that something has gone wrong with "the Code" and the related "popu-policy": aggression seems on the increase again, the heterosexual Professorials whom it has rendered marginal and socially deviant are so demoralized their crucial scientific work is suffering, and the surrogate mothers of the Clone children are beginning to resist the state command to surrender their children. We follow the interwoven experiences of four characters pinched by these increasingly dysfunctional scientific control strategies: Ric, the Council historian who has

173

fallen in love with a Clone boy and who is beginning to doubt the rightness of "the Code"; Miryam and Carlo, plant geneticists who are heterosexual, married, and worst of all parents of their own biological children; and Lilac, the Clone Mum who does not want to surrender her "beloved Ninety" for state conditioning.

Mitchison's intertwined plots dramatize the broad-ranging implications of science's effort to attain reproductive control and genetic/behavioral uniformity. Miryam and Carlo discover that the program of plant genetics to breed an increasingly narrow range of super-plants has begun to backfire. A flaw in the global crop of wheat and roses threatens the world's physical and emotional sustenance, for a virus has appeared that threatens to wipe out the entire genus unless variant species can be found. The two scientists must scramble to find wild roses and wild stands of wheat—varieties that have somehow survived despite, rather than because of, scientific efforts in plant breeding. The disaster-in-the-making teaches them that genetic diversity in plants is a biological principle that actively aids species survival.

In parallel developments, just as the other characters discover that the human sexual and social uniformity produced by "the Code" is as potentially dangerous as the genetic uniformity of the genus *rosaceae,* in Ulan Bator resentment against the privilege of the Clones reaches the boiling point and erupts into violence. Such a social crisis could, in another narrative, produce either bloody revolution or totalitarian crackdown. Indeed, both resulted in "Saunes Bairos," when Carila and Coraxi questioned the similarly repressive reproductive regime of the High Priests. But the society Mitchison imagines in *Solution Three* embodies not only feminist concerns, but feminist social and political practice. Faced with these challenges to "the Code," the Council responds not defensively but by welcoming the new voices and new perspectives they represent—because they catalyze growth, both in social relations and in scientific knowledge.

An interchange toward the end of *Solution Three* dramatizes this remarkable vision of a renewed, more inclusive government incorporating the insights of a revised, more collaborative science. Considering the recent violent uprisings in Ulan Bator, the crop failures, the changes in Clone sexuality, and the Clone Mums' defections from Council policy on child rearing, Head Councillor Matumba suggests that it may be time to reverse the scientific policy limiting reproduction to cloning, and thus controlling and limiting the gene pool. "But we can't just reverse a policy without landing the world in guilt and misery!" Councillor Jussie protests, reflecting the social and personal disorientation that follows from a paradigm shift. "That's not the way it should be done," replies Matumba. "Nor will it. None of us need be guilty. We have done right. But also we can change that right. Gently." (155)

Flexibility rather than rigidity, collaborative creation rather than competition, the acknowledgement that paradigms not only can but must shift in response to new voices and new needs: these qualities characterize the model for feminist scientific practice that Mitchison dramatizes in *Solution Three*. When the novel ends, as a result of this open vision of negotiated scientific and social practices, the genetically-grounded vision of reproduction and social life that has been "Solution Three" seems about to be replaced by a new, more diverse notion of the individual and society as subject to genetic, gestational, and environmental influences. This might be called "Solution Four." Mitchison has dramatized the benefits of a permeable science—a science that listens, responds, and accommodates to social forces—by showing how the scientifically-engaged Council of her future world builds in, rather than fights off, social critique.

As a work of literature, *Solution Three* shares the explicit engagement with problems of reproduction and child rearing that has animated feminist fictions from Charlotte Perkins Gilman's *Herland* (1915) to Katharine Burdekin's *Swastika Night* (1937) and Marge Piercy's *Woman on the Edge of Time* (1976). Like *Herland*, *Solution Three* imagines a society in which women have used reproductive control to shape a more equitable life for all, eradicating aggression and providing social support for motherhood. But if its vision of a society devoted to maternal values is familiar, its more positive vision of science seems unfamiliar, particularly in comparison to the masculinist dystopian science portrayed in a novel published just one year later, Marge Piercy's *Woman on the Edge of Time.*

Yet there is a precedent for Mitchison's feminist fascination with the world of science. As long ago as 1929, Virginia Woolf's brief glimpse of the modern novel in *A Room of One's Own* suggested the new possibilities for female friendship and collaboration that could be created by opening the realm of science to women. In *Life's Adventure,* by the fictitious Mary Carmichael, Chloe and Olivia share a laboratory together, mincing liver as a cure for pernicious anemia. Woolf's prototypical modern novel was modeled on *Love's Creation,* the scientifically informed novel published by Naomi Mitchison's family friend, birth control educator and paleontologist Dr. Marie Stopes, who used the pseudonym "Marie Carmichael."[30] Like *Love's Creation,* which Stopes claimed presented "the first publication of a large cosmic theory . . . a development of geological and paleontological researches," Mitchison's novel also presented the social implications of projected scientific findings, particularly investigations into the biological roots of aggression and techniques of genetic control.[31] Like Stopes's novel, *Solution Three* presents a new, more positive vision of science as a realm in which women could indeed make a difference and shape the course of knowledge. This new feminist vision of science, Woolf implicitly predicted in her narrative of Chloe and Olivia sharing a laboratory together, would play a central role in modern women's writing.

This dual engagement with science and feminism has been a mixed blessing when it comes to the reception of Mitchison's works. When I proposed to her that The Feminist Press reprint *Solution Three,* the letter I received in reply exhibited her characteristic mixture of scientific engagement and ironic populism: "It would be a great pleasure to have it reprinted," she told me. "I did swim in a lot of muddy waters with the book, but the nice thing is that it has been well liked by various good real scientists . . . I have always been more interested in the actual readers rather than publishers and rights! What was so pleasing was that some of them liked it a lot."[32] Yet if scientist and non-scientist readers alike enjoyed *Solution Three,* the reviewers were another, all too familiar, story. Once again, critics failed to appreciate Mitchison's feminist vision and seemed unable to understand the sweeping nature of her social critique. An excerpt from one particularly misguided review, in the *Times Literary Supplement,* epitomizes reviewers' failure to appreciate Mitchison's acute critique of even a feminist use of science to achieve the goal of a classless, non-sexist, non-racist world: "Naomi Mitchison's *Solution Three* is almost placid in its picture of a world gone sane.... The result is oddly appealing, rather like *Brave New World* (in its time) in combining a rejection of current mores with the retention of upper-class speech patterns and social graces."[33] With its challenge to all forms of patriarchal, class, and race privilege, and its critique of scientific control strategies even when waged on behalf of women, *Solution Three* is hardly likely to appeal to a journal as comfortably ensconced in white male privilege as was the *TLS* in 1975. Unless, that is, the reviewer completely misses the novel's import, which is clearly what happened. To compare Mitchison's novel to Huxley's *Brave New World* is a misunderstanding on many levels. It is unconvincing to compare Huxley's society, in which "Mother" is an obscenity, to Mitchison's vision of the social respect accorded to the Clone Mums. It is impossible to see a resemblance between the "pneumatic" Lenina Crowne and Mitchison's grave and thoughtful Matumba; between Bernard Marx or John the Savage and Ric the Council historian. But most of all it is unthinkable to find parallels between Huxley's world of "Our Ford," with its Soma-drugged populace, its Feelies, and its factory-engineered reproduction, and Solution Three's future world governed by a "Code" of careful nurturance and thoughtful social planning to eradicate violence and oppression.

Since she wrote *Solution Three,* science, social critique, and feminism have continued to ground Naomi Mitchison's vision of the world, even as the publishing world has become increasingly commercialized and the institution of science has become more and more the realm of High Priests rather than ordinary people. Indeed, changes in the publishing world may explain why *Solution Three* was never published in the United States and has been out of print in Great Britain since 1980. "As always, my best books don't get bought," Mitchison wrote me in 1990. "In fact I now find it difficult even to find a publisher."[34] "The problem about publishing now is that almost all the main publishers in England have been taken over by Americans who have different tastes."[35] Elsewhere, Mitchison amplified this point caustically:

> I write a number of different kinds of books, as you see. When I began writing this was possible because at that time books were written because the authors had something they wanted to say; today books are a commodity like other commodities. What is important is whether publishers think they can sell them. Most publishers have definite selling plans and if a given book does not fit into this, the author has little chance of getting it published. Today, if one wants to write about something special, one has to try and persuade a publisher that this was something he had already thought of.[36]

Mitchison has described her work to me as uncomfortably positioned between discursive fields: "Scientists think I am frivolous and non-scientists think I make things difficult."[37] Although that comment might in part explain why her science fiction writings have yet to develop the following they deserve, it also expresses a central source of strength in her fiction. Mitchison's habit of thinking across disciplinary boundaries is far from frivolous or *merely* difficult. A comment on current events in a letter written in 1991 can illustrate the complex and valuable ways Mitchison interweaves present and past, science, politics, and art to illuminate experience. She compared the effects of the Gulf War to World War I, which was the painful sequel of "Saunes Bairos":

> We are now suffering some of the edges of the last war. Much more will be lost if capitalism goes on, as it longs to take over everything (see, for instance the fight to keep it off the south pole). The way things are going now is almost too bad to write about. And all this nonsense about a war with nobody killed. Very few American and

British soldiers, no doubt, but thousands, probably millions of people in the countries of Asia Minor. . . . I think it would be too embarrassing to see Saunes Bairos in print again. And painful; almost all the young men who acted in it were killed in the first war, though my brother luckily escaped twice with wounds, my husband the same once. This last war did a lot more damage to animals including such things as corals and sea creatures than it did to humans.[38]

This letter shows the same, deeply felt, productive transgression of epistemological, social, and biological categories that links "Saunes Bairos" to *Solution Three*. Here, as in both of those works, Mitchison demonstrates her iconoclastic, serious, and productive feminist method of making things difficult. Using science to trouble social activism, and social activism to trouble science, she encourages us to extend the possibilities of both.

Susan M. Squier

Notes

1. Susan Squier, *Babies in Bottles: Twentieth-Century Visions of Reproductive Technology* (New Brunswick: Rutgers University Press, 1994).

2. N.M.M. Mitchison, two notebooks containing corrected drafts of "The Clone Mums," The National Library of Scotland, Edinburgh, Acc. 5831.

3. In fact, as I continued to read in the Mitchison papers, I discovered that the novel was drawn not only from scientific inspiration, but from her own eldest daughter's experiences traveling in Outer Mongolia. Naomi Mitchison, "Why Do We Write?" in Haldane papers, the National

Library of Scotland, Acc. 7219.

4. A virtual explosion of feminist scholarship exists concerning the new reproductive technologies. A crucial early work was Gena Corea, *The Mother Machine: Reproductive Technologies from Artificial Insemination to Artificial Wombs* (London: The Women's Press, 1988). Among the most thoughtful of the recent studies are: Marilyn Strathern, *Reproducing the Future: Anthropology, Kinship, and the New Reproductive Technologies* (London and New York: Routledge, 1992) and Michelle Stanworth, ed., *Reproductive Technologies: Gender, Motherhood and Medicine* (Minneapolis, Minn.: The University of Minnesota Press, 1987). For the most recent breakthrough on human cloning, see Boyce Rensberger, "Human Embryo Clones: Dividing Fact and Fiction," *The Journal of NIH Research,* January 1994, vol. 6, no. 1, 26–27, and Kathy A. Fackelmann, "Cloning Human Embryos," *Science News,* vol. 145, no. 6, February 5, 1994, 92–93, 95.

5. Jill Benton, *Naomi Mitchison: A Biography* (London: Pandora, 1990; rpt., 1992), 1–2. In my view, the rhyme of "Cloan" and "Clone" that surfaces with *Solution Three* confirms what the novel otherwise suggests: Mitchison's identificatory empathy with the painful situation of Lilac, the Clone Mum, who was faced with the requirement that she surrender her "beloved Ninety" to the State for conditioning. Following in the model set by her Haldane grandmother, Mitchison sent her own sons to boarding school, itself a form of frequently painful conditioning for upper-class British boys.

6. Naomi Mitchison, *Solution Three* (London: Dennis Dobson, 1975), jacket copy.

7. "The Huxleys were so nearly counted as kin that chaperonage was not considered necessary," Mitchison writes in "All Change Here: Girlhood and Marriage," *As It Was: An Autobiography: 1897–1918* (Glasgow: Richard Drew Publishing, 1975; rpt. 1988), 71. See also Benton, *Naomi Mitchison: A Biography*; Ronald Clark, *J.B.S.: The Life and Work of J.B.S. Haldane* (London: Hodder & Stoughton, 1968); and Gary Wersky, *The Visible College: A Collective Biography of British Scientists and Socialists of the 1930s*

(London: Free Association Books, 1988).

8. Mitchison, "Small Talk: Memories of an Edwardian Childhood," *As It Was,* 87.

9. Mitchison, "Small Talk," *As It Was,* 91; *You May Well Ask: A Memoir 1920–1940* (London: Fontana, 1986), 34. See also Benton, *Naomi Mitchison: A Biography.*

10. Benton, *Naomi Mitchison.*

11. Lesley Henderson, ed., *Contemporary Novelists* (Chicago and London: St. James Press, 1991), 646–648.

12. Benton, *Naomi Mitchison,* 150.

13. Mitchison, *Memoirs of a Spacewoman* (London: Victor Gollancz, 1962; rpt., New York: Berkeley, 1973) and *Not by Bread Alone* (London and Boston: Marion Boyars, 1983).

14. Mitchison, *The Conquered* (London: Cape, 1923); *Cloud Cuckoo Land* (London: Cape, 1925) and *The Corn King and the Spring Queen* (London: Cape, 1931; rpt., New York: Overlook, 1990).

15. Benton, *Naomi Mitchison,* 69.

16. Mitchison, *We Have Been Warned* (London: Constable & Co., 1935).

17. Mitchison, *You May Well Ask: A Memoir 1920–1940,* 172–181; Benton, *Naomi Mitchison,* 92–93.

18. Founded by statistician and Victorian amateur scientist Francis Galton, the Eugenics Education Society was dedicated to encouraging procreation among those it deemed more fit, and discouraging it among those it deemed less fit. Daniel J. Kevles, *In the Name of Eugenics: Genetics and the Uses of Human Heredity* (Berkeley: The University of California Press, 1985).

19. Katharine Burdekin, *Swastika Night* (London: Victor Gollancz, 1937; rpt., with an introduction by Daphne Patai, New York: The Feminist Press, 1985).

20. A newspaper article (source unknown) entitled "Clever Amateurs at Oxford" reported, "The performance went very briskly, and the young authoress, at the end, met with a well-merited ovation," while another article entitled "City and Country Topics" not only mentioned the

"enthusiastic ovation" and "a great presentation of bouquets," but observed, "The play is certainly a work of great promise." Press clippings, origin unknown, Acc. 6213, in the Mitchison papers, National Library of Scotland, Edinburgh.

21. Helen Cooke, 23 Linton Road, Oxford, to Mrs. Haldane, Cherwell, 8 May 1913, in the Haldane collection, National Library of Scotland, Acc. 4549, 1–9. Paragraphing removed. In "All Change Here," Mitchison recalls that Mary Cooke was the "niece of J.A.R. Marriott, at one time Conservative candidate for the University [Oxford]," whose mother was "quite a talented painter" (*As It Was,* 13).

22. Mitchison, "Small Talk," *As It Was,* 23–24.

23. Mitchison, "All Change Here," *As It Was,* 61, 63.

24. Quoted in Mitchison, "All Change Here," *As It Was,* 63.

25. Mitchison, "All Change Here," 61, 63.

26. See Evelyn Fox Keller, "Making Gender Visible in the Pursuit of Nature's Secrets," in Teresa de Lauretis, ed., *Feminist Studies/Critical Studies* (Bloomington: Indiana University Press, 1986), 67–77.

27. Shulamith Firestone, *The Dialectic of Sex* (New York: William Morrow and Co., 1970; rpt., Bantam Books, 1971), 206.

28. Dorothy Dinnerstein, *The Mermaid and the Minotaur: Sexual Arrangements and Human Malaise* (New York: Harper Colophon, 1977), 33 (capitalization removed), and Nancy Chodorow, *The Reproduction of Mothering: Psychoanalysis and the Sociology of Gender* (Berkeley: University of California Press, 1978).

29. See the essays in Marianne Hirsch and Evelyn Fox Keller, eds., *Conflicts in Feminism* (New York: Routledge, 1990).

30. Lesley A. Hall, "Uniting Science and Sensibility: Marie Stopes and the Narratives of Marriage in the 1920s," in Angela Ingram and Daphne Patai, eds., *Rediscovering Forgotten Radicals: British Women Writers 1889–1939* (Chapel Hill: The University of North Carolina Press, 1993), 118–136.

31. Hall, "Uniting Science and Sensibility," *Rediscovering Forgotten Radicals,* 126.

32. Mitchison, personal letter to the author, November 29, 1991.

33. T. A. Shippey, "Spenserian Future," Times Literary Supplement, 5 December 1975, 1438.

34. Mitchison, personal correspondence to the author, April 9, 1990.

35. Mitchison, personal correspondence to the author, May 29, 1990.

36. Lesley Henderson, ed., *Contemporary Novelists* (Chicago and London: St. James's Press, 1991), 646–648.

37. Mitchison, personal letter to the author, April 9, 1990.

38. Mitchison, personal letter to the author, October 25, 1991.

The Feminist Press at The City University of New York offers alternatives in education and in literature. Founded in 1970, this nonprofit, tax-exempt educational and publishing organization works to eliminate stereotypes in books and schools and to provide literature with a broad vision of human potential. The publishing program includes reprints of important works by women, feminist biographies of women, multicultural anthologies, a cross-cultural memoir series, and nonsexist children's books. Curricular materials, bibliographies, directories, and a quarterly journal provide information and support for students and teachers of women's studies. Through publications and projects, The Feminist Press contributes to the rediscovery of the history of women and the emergence of a more humane.

New and Forthcoming Books

Always a Sister: The Feminism of Lillian D. Wald. A biography by Doris Groshen Daniels. $12.95, paper.

The Answer/La Respuesta (Including a Selection of Poems), by Sor Juana Inés de la Cruz. Critical Edition and translation by Electa Arenal and Amanda Powell. $12.95 paper, $35.00 cloth.

Black and White Sat Down Together: The Reminiscences of an NAACP Founder, by Mary White Ovington. Edited and with a foreword by Ralph E. Luker. Afterword by Carolyn E. Wedin. $19.95 cloth.

Challenging Racism and Sexism: Alternatives to Genetic Explanations (Genes and Gender VII). Edited by Ethel Tobach and Betty Rosoff. $14.95 paper, $35.00 cloth.

China for Women: Travel and Culture. $17.95, paper.

Music and Women, by Sophie Drinker. Afterword by Ruth A. Solie. $16.95, paper, $37.50, cloth.

No Sweetness Here, by Ama Ata Aidoo. Afterword by Ketu Katrak. $10.95, paper, $29.00, cloth.

Streets: A Memoir of the Lower East Side. By Bella Spewack. Introduction by Ruth Limmer. Afterword by Lois Elias. $19.95, cloth.

Prices subject to change. Individuals: Send check or money order (in U.S. dollars drawn on a U.S. bank) to The Feminist Press at The City University of New York, 311 East 94th Street, New York, NY 10128. Please include $4.00 postage and handling for the first book, $1.00 for each additional. For VISA/MasterCard orders call (212) 360-5790. Bookstores, libraries, wholesalers: Feminist Press titles are distributed to the trade by Consortium Book Sales and Distribution, (800) 283-3572.